Copyright © 2006 Sapphirefly, 2019 Stephanie Van Orman

All right reserved. No part of this book may be reproduced or used in any manner without written permission of the copyright owner except for the use of written quotations in a book review.

Any reference to historical events, real people or places are used fictitiously. Names, characters, places are products of the author's imagination.

Front cover image by Kaitlynn Van Orman
Book Design by Stephanie Van Orman
Author photograph by Alison Quist

First printing edition 2019
stephanievanorman.blogspot.com

Whenever You Want

Stephanie Van Orman

For my favorite beta reader, Kat Thornton

Chapter One

A Request for Tina

Christina Witten placed the final double red lines at the end of the last column on her accounting exam. She flipped her test booklet to the front to make sure her student information was correct and then she gathered her things together. She felt a certain relief as she saw she was not the first person to finish the test and not anywhere near the last. It was comfortable for her to finish sometime in the middle. All her numbers matched, so it had to be good enough. She turned in her exam, swung her bag over her shoulder and headed for the door.

It was a weight off her mind! The test had been an important one. The last one in April—end game. Once she got her (hopefully) good grades back, she'd have her diploma in office assistance and she could quit living her secret life. Not many girls lived a secret life, but if anyone back home heard she'd been working for an escort service, that would be the end of her freedom. She knew for certain her parents would pitch an epic fit and she'd be back in her home town pumping gas before she could say, "No tuition."

It hadn't been Christina's idea to work for an escort service. Well, it hadn't been her idea in the first place, but when her cousin Mindy showed her how much money could be made by being the shiny little woman on a boring man's arm for one evening… poor little Christina had to cave. Her pockets were worn thin. She needed money.

It was all because of her own stupidity that she had been short on cash. She was the one who told her parents she had enough money to leave her small town and move to faraway Edmonton. It didn't matter how far away she went, they didn't have any money to help her even if she lived next door, but she wasn't worried. She could take care of everything. She always planned to get a part-time job to help support herself while she went to school, but then she'd been late turning in a form to request a grant and even later with her application for a scholarship. In the end, it didn't seem to matter how many dishes she washed at the pub around the corner, there was barely enough money to pay the rent as well as her tuition. Feeding herself became a problem, too, and though Christina didn't like to say it—she'd already maxed out her credit card buying food and those expensive textbooks.

    She often wondered if she should have told Mindy about her money problems before they got out of hand, but Mindy was very different from her and the only reason Christina's parents had allowed her move to Edmonton in the first place. She had to live with responsible Mindy who was making a killing at her job… which was? Christina was very suspicious. Mindy was hardly ever home in the evenings and wherever she went, she dolled up like a celebrity about to strut down the red carpet. What could she be doing? At first, Mindy blubbered something about networking. She didn't give any details about her career until Christina broke down and explained she was fifty dollars short on her half of the rent that month. She'd been killing herself at work for three months and she thought Mindy would understand if she was a little late.

    Mindy looked at the money that wasn't quite enough and then at Christina before she said, "Your arms looked chapped. Do you want to make some money at something that doesn't involve elbow-deep boiling water?"

"But that's my job," Christina responded dully, almost on the point of tears.

"It doesn't have to be," Mindy said, dropping the bills Christina gave her on the table like they were nothing. She clicked over to the refrigerator in her high heels and took out a can of tonic water, which she opened noisily before leaning against the wall of their apartment like she was marketing the stuff. "I could take you to work with me, and you'd earn enough to pay your tuition for next semester in a couple weeks, especially since Christmas is coming up. You see, I'm actually—"

"A hooker?" Christina filled in for her.

"*Escort*!" Mindy emphasized. Then she shrugged her shoulders. "It's not even that bad."

"So, you don't sleep with them?"

"My clients? Ew! No," Mindy said, looking repulsed. "Not in a million years. But I do go on dates with guys who need a date for something and don't have the time or inclination to find a date for themselves. Sometimes, it's because they're shy. Sometimes, it's because they want to make a girl who's slighted them off burn with envy. Sometimes, it's because they're visiting the city and want someone to show them around with a little more intimacy than a touring bus. Stuff like that. Very often, they introduce me as their cousin." Mindy explained before she bluntly asked Christina, "Well, do you want to try it?"

"No sex?" Christina asked anxiously.

"Zero sex. I promise. I'll give you pepper spray and a pair of brass knuckles. Want to give it a try?"

"Aren't both of those illegal?"

"Probably," Mindy said noncommittally. "I've never been attacked. I don't know what happens with other escort services, but my agency's really good. We're professionals and we say what we are willing to do very clearly in our ads. Gross stuff just doesn't happen."

"I'll think about it," Christina said.

"Do," Mindy said. "Do."

So, Christina thought about it. She didn't have much of a choice. She didn't have enough money to pay the tuition for the next semester and it would be due in mere weeks. If she could earn the money she needed, then she could quit being an escort and go back to washing dishes. If she refused the job, she'd probably have to drop out of her program and go back home. That would be too humiliating. On the other hand, could she really be an escort?

Christina thought honestly about Mindy and how she compared. Mindy was shorter than Christina unless she was wearing battle gear. When she was all dressed for work, Mindy wore ten-centimeter heels. She was tanned and pierced and tattooed in all the right places and Christina was simply nothing like her.

Christina didn't even have long, pretty hair. Her hair was that unfortunate color that was neither blonde or brown, and to top it off, it was cropped so short that it was almost boyish. She had no figure to speak of. She was pale and... ordinary. Couldn't a guy get a girl like her anywhere?

"Don't you think I'm plain?" Christina asked when Mindy broached the subject a second time.

"Plain?" Mindy asked skeptically. "Plain? What do you mean? If you think you're ugly, think again. It's true, you need help, but your problems are nothing that can't be solved with makeup and a little extra attention. Basically, if you give me permission to do whatever it takes to bring you up to snuff, you'll look like a fox promptly."

"Really?"

Mindy snuffed, "Everything is fake anyway."

"No one is naturally beautiful?"

Mindy rolled her eyes and said caustically, "Even Cinderella needed a glass shoe."

"Then I'll do it," Christina said. She was too desperate to pay her bills to think rationally.

"Okay then. You asked for it," Mindy said, picking up her car keys and heading for the door.

Mindy took Christina to her agency where she introduced her to the boss and told her they could use her for the busy season. No one wanted to be alone around Christmas time, so there was always more than enough work. The woman in charge didn't seem very interested in Christina, but assigned her the working name of 'Tina' and told her she'd work with Mindy the first few times just to make sure she was trained properly. Then Mindy took her to the back for her makeover.

The first thing Mindy did once they were alone was pierce Christina's ears. She'd never had it done and it felt like her head was going to explode it hurt so much.

Mindy groaned when Christina whined. "Look, I'm not going to brand you. It's a miracle you managed to make it to nineteen without having it done anyway. This isn't a big deal."

But, it didn't matter what Mindy said, Christina still felt sore as Mindy busily gave her a facial, manicure, pedicure, plucked her eyebrows and did her makeup.

When Mindy finally left her alone, she felt sure she'd made the wrong choice. Beauty was too painful for her. She didn't want to be beautiful when the price was getting your eyebrows plucked—hair by hair. She even considered bolting… but she did need the money. Ugh! She had to endure it.

Mindy brought her back a long honey colored wig and plopped it on her head happily.

"It's great that your hair is so short. This way we can do whatever we want with you," she said with a smile. "You're going to be super hot."

All in all, by the time Mindy was truly finished with Christina she was living a double life. By day, she was mild mannered college student Christina Witten and by evening she was Tina, an extremely beautiful and elusive escort who would never be seen past Christmas.

Or so she thought.

Mindy was right. Christmas was busy. Tina went to six office Christmas parties, three charity auctions, one ball, two shopping excursions, a dinner party, and a performance of *The Nutcracker*. By Boxing Day, her first day off, she looked at how much money she'd earned dating *interesting* men, and she was still four hundred dollars short on tuition, not to mention January's rent, and additional expenses. She crunched the notice in her hand and knew exactly what it meant. She would have to work on New Year's Eve. And who would be her partner that evening?

So far, the guys she had dated hadn't seemed that bad. Most of them were in their twenties or thirties. They didn't have wives and weren't likely to. They had just gotten in the habit of phoning for a date when one of these once-a-year awkward occasions came up. Some were more embarrassed than others, but she worked hard to make them all feel like she saw them as real people instead of just a customer. One of them even phoned and requested her again. Mindy thought that was great and gave Christina smiles and cheek pinches to congratulate her on her first return client.

When the end of the night came with one of these men, they'd call a cab for her and put her in it without asking for so much as a hug. More than one of them had even told her that she was much too good a girl to be working as an escort and she'd be better off giving it up.

But by Boxing Day, she hadn't earned enough money and she'd have to work New Year's Eve—terrifying.

Mindy's words still haunted her. "New Year's Eve," she said with a wink. "Everybody's date gets a kiss on New Year's Eve. Don't even think of trying to skip out."

Christina gulped. If she worked that night, she'd definitely have to kiss her date!

***

Christina popped her purple bubblegum and tried to work out some of the tension in her back. It was the dreaded night—New Year's Eve. Rats! She was dressed like two billion dollars. Her dress was deep red, the color of the season, and she was wearing a long black coat with fur trimming Mindy had loaned her for the occasion. All her clothes were borrowed from Mindy, except for the inserts in her bra (those were a gift). To complete her look, Christina wore long dangling earrings with rhinestones inset in them and a choker to match. The wrap she would wear once the coat was hung up was black with deep red blossoms scattered across it in a gorgeous array. Christina thought it was prettier than the dress. The wig she wore that night was sandy blonde with bangs that fell slightly into her eyes.

That night she was supposed to meet Mr. Mark Lewis in the lobby of the Grand Morton Hotel—downtown—uptown—a really good part of town. There was a party there in one of the ballrooms and she was his insurance that he wouldn't be going stag to the biggest party of the year.

She pushed through the revolving doors just before eight o'clock hoping she'd find him quickly. She was supposed to wait by the courtesy phone in the lobby. Phase one of the date wasn't a big deal. She'd been meeting men that way all along. Even though it had barely been a month, she felt like a seasoned professional. The reason sweat was forming in the space between her shoulder blades was that she couldn't stop thinking about the cold fact that she was going to have to kiss her date. Of course, Mindy was right. Having someone to kiss at the stroke of midnight was the whole purpose of hiring an escort on New Year's Eve. It was socially embarrassing to have no one to kiss. Christina just needed to pull herself together. She'd been kissed before. Lots of times... she thought.

She rolled her eyes and looked around for a place to spit her gum before her date got there. But she was so nervous she accidentally started to blow another bubble.

"Looking for something?" a deep male voice said coolly.

Christina's gum bubble deflated as her eyes met those of one of the most handsome men she had ever seen. Christina didn't even get a chance to examine him closely when she realized he was holding a silver dust bin in his hand, poised to catch her gum.

Christina reached into her pocket and quickly pulled out a tissue. There was no way that guy was her date, but her date was probably in the lobby (if he was on time) and she didn't want him to see her spit a wad of purple bubble gum directly into a waste bin. She already felt like she'd tripped up by being majorly outclassed in the fancy hotel. She rolled her gum up in the Kleenex and dropped it into the bin.

"Thank you," she said, trying to cool her cheeks and manage some sort of composure. Then she moved away and stood closer to the courtesy phone. She leaned against the pillar and tried to look for her date.

But the guy with the trash can wasn't leaving. He set the bin down near a chair, came around, and leaned against the pillar beside her. "Was your gum grape or raisin flavored?"

"Those are the same," Christina said, still scanning the room and not looking at the man next to her. "It just depends on whether or not the French side of the package is showing."

He laughed. "Are you waiting for somebody?" he asked, flirting.

"I have a date."

"Is he handsome?"

"Who?"

"Your date," he answered, chuckling.

Christina looked around nervously. She had never seen the man. How was she supposed to answer? The stranger was clearly playing with her. If she said her date was gorgeous, she'd be in trouble when the short, bald guy rolled in. After scrambling for a moment, she answered, "I like the way he looks."

"Hmm," the brown-eyed stranger said, as he suddenly turned around the corner and put his arm by her shoulder, nearly pinning her against the pillar. "And you're friendly with him no doubt?"

She nodded and said testily, "That's why you shouldn't be putting the moves on me."

"Mark!" someone suddenly called from the other end of the lobby. It was a silver tinkling voice, exactly like the sound of Christmas ornaments jingling.

Christina turned her head to see who had called her date's first name, when suddenly the stranger in front of her closed in and whispered, "Sorry for the late introduction. I'm Mark and I'm guessing you're my date. Tina? Am I right?"

"Yeah," Christina breathed, very much aware of his cologne. Breathing it in was a new sensation. What on earth was he wearing? But Christina still had the presence of mind to say, "But you're not behaving very well. Do you have to stand that close to me?"

"I need you to help me with a little problem," he said, taking her hand in his and leading her toward the woman who had called to him. He held onto her hand and introduced her to a ravishing blonde.

Her name was Laura. It was only necessary to take one look at her to learn that she was eating her heart out for Christina's date.

"Don't you ever go out with the same woman twice?" Laura asked poisonously when Mark slipped his arm around Christina's waist.

Christina smiled and looked at him. Yeah, he definitely looked like the heart-breaker type. She was smiling though, because she was happy he had turned out to be her partner for the night. She couldn't help it. So far, none of her dates had been with men that were above an average on an attractive-o-meter. Mark was undoubtedly a ten on any woman's rating chart. At least she wouldn't have to kiss someone at the end of the night she was not attracted to. So, she was smiling and enjoying the fun of being with a man who was obviously popular. Mindy had already prepared her for being a tool to make another woman jealous.

"Don't scare Tina," Mark said to Laura sternly.

"But I know how you like to give your flings the idea that it's not just a fling," she said, looking particularly wounded. "Someone needs to warn the poor girl."

Christina smiled and answered before Mark had a chance to say anything. "Thanks for the warning, but I'm too young to settle down. You should just enjoy the moment. Don't you think?" Even Christina thought her cheerful eyes and ringing voice were irritating as she said those words. Saying a line like that irked her conscience, even as she said it. She didn't believe it at all. She wanted a steady boyfriend who wouldn't just use her for a fling, but for a long life of deep, lasting love. However, Mark was paying her to be on his side, so she said what she had to without choking on her own tongue.

Christina knew she was successful when Laura gave her a disgusted look and then beckoned for someone across the room to join them. "He'll make you sorry, even if you have that attitude," she said crossly as she took the arm of a young man. He was tall and blond and Christina might have been mistaken, but she thought Laura's date looked at her a trifle longer than was necessary.

Christina flashed a smile back at him. It was all part of leading her secret life. Smiling sweetly at strangers was all part of being Tina. Well, she wouldn't have to do it for much longer. New Year's was going to be the last night. Afterward, she'd have to make up the difference washing dishes in the back of the pub again. Maybe then she could relax because no one would ever find out what she'd been doing.

Mark led her over to the coat check and politely helped her remove her coat. "You really riled her up," he said as he offered her an arm and led her down the stairs to the ballroom.

"Is she your ex-girlfriend?" Christina asked, trying to get a grasp of the situation. Maybe he would tell her.

"Not exactly. More like a hopeful girlfriend," he explained.

Man alive! He had excellent posture. Christina pushed her shoulders back and tried to walk with half as much dignity as him. Having to match a guy like him was daunting, but she'd do her best. "And this is your way of letting her down easy?" Christina asked.

"Sort of," Mark agreed, turning his dark eyes toward her.

"Did you have a fling with her?"

Mark looked annoyed, but it didn't make him look like an ogre. With features like that, he couldn't stop being gorgeous even with a scowl on his face. Even his arm was solid.

"I don't think that's any of your business," he finally replied. "I said I need you to help me with something tonight and it wasn't her. I assure you, I can take care of that situation myself. There's something else. Last year, at the New Year's party, I had some… unpleasantness at midnight. You're going to keep me out of trouble. All right?"

Christina smiled and promised she'd do a good job.

***

All in all, the evening was oceans more fun than she expected. She danced with Mark most of the time, and when he was called away by someone else, she danced with one of his friends. He had nice friends. They were good looking, young, successful, and didn't have wandering hands when they danced with her. The food was excellent and Mark was a good date. He was clearly popular both in his profession and with his friends, because he introduced her to at least fifty people, if not more. He had a good sense of fun and knew how to dance. He told her about his interests in a way that none of her other dates had bothered to. It was almost like he wasn't sure how to date an escort and so he was dating her in the same way he would date her if he was really interested in her. By the end of the night, she thought more than once that it was a pity her date with Mark was just for her job; otherwise, she would have loved to find herself in a more long-term relationship with him.

At around eleven-thirty, he gave up leaving her even for a moment. He took hold of her hand tightly while they danced and turned people down if they tried to take her from him by cutting in.

"What happened last year that makes you so nervous about midnight?" she asked while pressed close to him in a dance.

He rolled his eyes. "I'd rather not talk about it. It was… unpleasant."

"You keep using that word!"

"Yeah, well, it was. Fine, I'll tell you. I ended up getting passed down a long line of women and it was… unpleasant," he said, looking like he still needed to wash his mouth out.

"I thought most guys would like that." She laughed.

"Are you kidding? It was so fast I didn't even get a chance to recognize all of them. No, it wasn't fun."

"Yeah, I know it was… unpleasant. And this year, I'm supposed to protect you from it?"

"Well, don't tell me you don't think I look great in my dinner jacket, so…" he paused. Then he leaned in, put his forehead against Christina's, and looked into her eyes. "Please take care of me."

Christina wasn't sure, but she thought knowing she was going to get to kiss him at midnight was making it even more exciting. She looked at the giant clock at the end of the hall. Sometimes it seemed to be moving faster and sometimes it seemed to be moving slower. In a minute the countdown would start.

"Ten!"

"Nine!"

"Eight!"

"Seven!"

Mark turned Christina toward him and put his arms around her waist. She was looking into his eyes. She couldn't even hear the noise of the crowd filling the ballroom. There was just her and him.

And then their kiss.

The room was stifling, and so his lips were hot as he pressed them down on hers. Christina had told herself over and over again she had been kissed plenty of times, and so it wasn't a big deal, but kissing Mark was different. She had never felt her blood like it was scorching through her veins. It was like she was being kissed by someone who knew how to kiss, by someone who really meant business, and by someone who was not going to let up. It wasn't the kiss of a passing stranger who just wanted to avoid being passed around. Instead, it seemed like the kiss of someone who wanted something badly but was not allowed to have it. Christina broke away and took a quick breath. He pulled her back roughly. Her brain was shutting down, but she had one more thought before she completely shut down. She thought that to him, she must seem like the type of woman who wasn't attainable. Since kissing her was a once-in-a-lifetime opportunity, he wouldn't stop.

And she didn't really want him to.

At some point, Christina somehow became aware the singing had stopped and the band had stopped playing. Christina put her hand to Mark's face and pulled off. Then she looked into his eyes and smiled like their kiss had been part of the act. "Did I do a good job guarding your honor?" she asked with a wicked smile.

His expression went blank like he just realized what was going on. Maybe, his expression was of disappointment, because he just remembered she really wasn't attainable.

"Of course," he said. "You did a great job. Do you want something to drink?"

She nodded and he strode toward the bar.

Christina went back to their table and sat down. Why did she have to ruin everything by reminding him she was only an escort? They could have enjoyed the fantasy for another couple of hours, couldn't they?

Mark returned and gave her a glass of soda water—the only thing she had been drinking all night. He sat down next to her, his expression black when suddenly he was grabbed from behind and given a kiss on the mouth by a woman. It wasn't Laura, but someone else. Christina put a hand to her forehead and wanted to groan. There was no way she could have stopped someone that fast.

Afterward, the woman winked at Christina and said, "It's just not New Year's without kissing Mark!"

Mark didn't smile, and Christina was worried he might be mad at her. Instead, he ran a hand through his hair and leaned forward to ask pleasantly, "Could I please have a piece of your grape bubblegum?"

Christina smiled. "Sorry, I only have raisin."

"Please," he persisted. "I gotta get that taste out of my mouth, and I already used your token kiss for the evening. Please?"

She clicked open her purse and pulled out a piece of gum. After unwrapping it for him, she popped it into his mouth.

"It's too bad this is just for tonight," she said, "because if it was just you and me with no strings attached… I know I'd fall for you." She reflected later she never could have said those words if she didn't have the cover of her identity as Tina. Because she was playing Tina, she was able to say something that daring. Christina never played coy.

"I'll bet you say that to everyone," he said, before biting down hard on the gum.

She smiled. "Didn't you enjoy hearing it?"

Then he pulled her to her feet and made her dance with him.

Chapter Two

Two Requests?

After New Year's Eve, Christina went back to washing dishes in the back of her pub for the month of January and tried not to think about what she could be missing working as an escort. After all, not every date had been like the last one with Mark Lewis. Yup! She didn't think about what Mark's kiss had been like or how he held her while they danced. She didn't think about his eyes or the way his hair fell into them. Nope! Not one bit!

Best of all, she didn't think about the money she was missing out on while she worked her *honest* minimum wage job. At least, not until her January paycheck came in. When she saw the numbers and did the accounting in her head, she computed just one fact—she was in trouble.

Mindy was reading a magazine in her recliner when Christina limped into the apartment after getting her pay stub. Mindy instantly flipped the glossy cover shut and took her headphones out of her ears to ask Christina, "So, how was work? Did you get paid?"

"I got paid," Christina sulked.

"Not enough?" Mindy inquired as she put her arms behind her head and stretched her body out. "You already owe me six hundred and twenty bucks and that's on top of February's rent. Do you think you're going to be able to make good? I'd hate to have to call Auntie and ask her to make up the difference for you. I can't pay for this place by myself."

"Yes, you can!" Christina countered noisily. Mindy made tons of money. She was just trying to bully Christina into going back to the escort service. "You could easily pay for this place by yourself."

"Ah," Mindy said. She sounded bored. "I suppose that's true, but I can't think of a good reason why I *should* have to pay for your housing when I have such good plans for my hard-earned money."

"I could pay you back!" Christina claimed.

"When?"

"After graduation—"

"Whatever," Mindy interrupted. "I'm not telling you what to do. You can get the money to pay me however you want and I guess whenever you want. I'm not heartless enough to call your parents and insist that they pay me. I just wanted to tell you that Valentine's Day is coming up and there has been a request for you through the agency."

"Really?"

"Yeah. A request for Tina! Do you feel like doing it?"

"What's the hourly rate for the job?" Christina asked. Not all jobs paid the same. She had made thirty dollars an hour during the Christmas holidays, except for New Year's and Christmas Eve. On those nights she had made fifty dollars an hour. "Valentine's is worth how much?"

"Fifty," Mindy said. "Except that there has been a miraculous turn of events in your favor. There wasn't just one request, but two."

"Two?" Christina asked, stunned. "What happens when there are two?"

"Well, you can either go out with the highest bidder, or you can go out with the one you like, or you can go with the one who made their appointment first, or whatever. You can flip a coin if you want. Feel like working?"

Christina crossed her fingers and said, "If either of those guys is Mark Lewis, I'll go on the date."

Mindy's eyes lit up. "That's a charming development! We're not supposed to have favorite clients, but it's inevitable. I have some I like better, but I'm probably more mercenary than you are. I like the ones that pay more."

"Was Mark one of them?" Christina asked impatiently.

"Yes, he was."

"YES!" Christina cheered with her arms in the air. "I'll go! Yay!"

"Wait, Darling," Mindy continued. "Get off the ceiling and listen to the rest. Hey!" she yelled, to get Christina's attention. "Sit down!"

Christina forced herself to sit cross-legged on the floor, but her cheeks were burning. She was so excited she was practically bouncing. Another date with Mark! Hooray!

"Calm yourself. Mark has only offered to pay the standard fee because he was the one to make the appointment before the other guy called and you got double booked. The other guy said he wanted you, too. So, we asked him if he was willing to outbid your first request for that night."

"Did you book me not knowing whether or not I'd be able to come in?" Christina questioned, feeling like she knew the answer before Mindy told her.

Her cousin winked. "Naturally. I didn't take you off the books. You still owe me money."

Christina groaned and Mindy went on.

"Anyway, he offered one hundred dollars an hour—into your pocket."

"A hundred dollars... an hour! You must be joking. A guy does not pay that much without expecting sex!" Christina exclaimed.

"This guy does. When he offered that much, the rules were firmly explained to him and he said he wanted you for a date and nothing more."

"Have I met this guy before? Did I go on a date with him?"

"I don't think so. He said he saw you at the New Year's Eve party. I guess your date was with Mark that night? Anyway, he thought you were interesting and he wants to take you out. His name is Dominic Figura. So, which will it be?"

Christina shrugged. "I'd rather date Mark, but that's a lot of money. Does he only want me for an hour then? Could I go to both?"

Mindy shook her head. "If memory serves—both of them wanted from seven to midnight. So, pulling a doubleheader is out of the question, but I'm proud of you for asking. You've got a dirty mind after all, don't you, Tina?"

"Shut up! I'm trying to make money here!"

"Then date Dominic. You'll make twice as much and cover five hundred dollars of your debt to me in one night. Even making a hundred dollars an hour, that won't even cover half of what you'll owe me by then. I'll tell you what I'd do. I'd date Dominic, stop being little miss goody-two-shoes, and work for the agency until you get a real job. That way you'll be out of debt when you graduate and you can move forward in your life with pride."

"You just want me to swallow my pride for now?" Christina asked, feeling heavy.

"Everyone should do it a time or two," she said before she claimed she needed a shower and left the room.

Christina sat alone in the living room. She felt flat. She really wanted to go on a date with Mark on Valentine's Day, but crappity-crap-crap-crap, she'd have to bail. She needed the money too much to take an opportunity like a hundred dollars an hour for granted. But, if she turned him down, would he ever call and request her again? She doubted it.

Yep! She was right the first time. She was in trouble.

***

Valentine's Day.

Even before the date, Christina felt sure she was already dead and roasting for her sins in hell, but how could she have known that Dominic would take her to the same restaurant as Mark that night? Bah!

Christina hadn't been the one to call Mark to tell him he had been outbid. Christina fed herself all kinds of good reasons why she had turned him down. She was doing it for the money, so why not do it for the money? If that was her philosophy, then it didn't matter who asked her. The sooner she could pay off Mindy and her credit card, the better. It wasn't like she wanted luxurious living. Mostly what she wanted was a reasonable meal. Eating cheap Asian noodles two meals a day was hardly nourishing, but she didn't have money for anything better.

She also told herself maybe it was better if it didn't go any further with Mark. It wasn't like he was going to fall head-over-heels for an escort, and the last thing she wanted was to fall in love with a guy who only thought of her as a purchased woman. It wasn't like she blamed him. When she was Tina, she was only a shade better than a prostitute. It was her job to make him comfortable and treat him like she liked him. It was all a game, so she couldn't blame him if he liked to play it, or stop playing when it suited him.

When she met Dominic in the lounge of the restaurant, she thought she had seen him before. New Year's Eve? That was when Mindy said they had met, but she couldn't place him. Dominic was blond and thin with a curious smile. He had a gleam in his eyes that couldn't be mistaken for anything except mischievousness. It must really be a game for him. Something about the arrangement must be extensively amusing. He was young and Christina wondered why he wasn't able to get a date on his own. He was handsome enough for it, but it didn't take her long to figure out why he had called and offered so much for her to accompany him that night—he was the Devil.

"I thought we'd have dinner with my sister and her boyfriend," he said, his eyes virtually on fire. "Afterward, we're going to see a movie."

That surprised Christina. A hundred dollars an hour to go watch a movie? Who paid for that? However, she took his arm and went with him into the dining room. His smile was as broad as a Cheshire cat. He was having *way* too much fun.

As she stepped onto the padded carpet, she saw Mark seated in a booth. He was wearing a dinner jacket similar to the one he had been on New Year's Eve, but his jacket wasn't done up and he wasn't wearing a tie.

Seated beside him was the woman he'd introduced to her—Laura. Then Christina remembered where she'd seen Dominic. He was the guy who was with Laura. Christina had given him a flirty smile and he paused. Mercy! Why had she smiled at him? She was definitely in trouble because Laura was Dominic's sister and Christina would be spending the evening watching Mark date her. Didn't Dominic say Mark and Laura were going out? Just peachy!

She shook out her fake hair and reminded herself that none of it mattered to her. She was playing the escort for the money and oddly enough, also for a free meal. She'd carry herself with poise and dignity. It wasn't like she had to explain anything to him. There was nothing to explain.

Christina sat down in the booth and scooted over so Dominic could sit next to her.

Actually, even though Christina told herself all that jargon about how she was dating Dominic for the money when she sat down and Dominic introduced her to his sister and Mark like they didn't know each other—she was distinctly uncomfortable.

"We've already met," Mark and Laura said at exactly the same moment. Mark looked away. He bit his cheek and tapped his fingers on the tablecloth.

Laura had more presence of mind and said to Dominic rudely, "I didn't realize you had such... thrilling taste in women."

Christina smiled. It was difficult, but she managed it. It was hell on earth, but on the bright side—at least Christina was dressed for it. Mindy had made her up for Valentine's Day herself, which meant that Christina was flawless. She was wearing a curly white-blonde wig with strawberry blonde highlights. It was so long, it hit her mid-back. Her dress was baby pink with white lace and she was wearing a white heart necklace. When Mindy put the cherry-red lipstick on, Christina thought her appearance was little better than cosplay.

"Don't be stupid," Mindy said angrily while she applied the top gloss to Christina's lips. "Men like long hair, pink dresses, heart-shaped necklaces, and white lace, and do you know why?"

"No," Christina answered meekly. It wasn't so bad to have Mindy teach her a thing or two even if she was snarly.

"Because men don't wear them," Mindy snapped. "He's paying one hundred dollars an hour for you, and you'd better make him feel like a man. But since I know you're so inexperienced, I can't count on you to take charge, so we have to do as much as we can with your appearance. Our agency's name is at stake. Don't blow it!"

Christina sat at the table thinking. If men liked pink and white lace, then Laura was toast. She was wearing a little black dress—perfect for almost any occasion—except for Valentine's Day. As for Christina, she knew that normally she'd fail at almost everything to do with feminine charm, but she had an ace up her sleeve—Mindy.

Christina had a surge of confidence once she remembered her darling cousin's tutoring. She'd make it a killer night. She'd make Dominic a fantastic date and be so good to him she'd make Mark want to flip the bill for her next time.

The menus came and Christina looked it over with pleasure. Finally, she'd get to have something good to eat.

"What would you like, Tina?" Dominic asked pleasantly.

Christina smiled back at him. He was definitely the devil. He was enjoying the awkwardness of the situation so much. Not only did he like to mess with Mark's brain, by outbidding him for the escort he wanted, but he also clearly liked making his sister uncomfortable as well.

Christina bit the corner of her lip. "Mm, everything looks so good. Could you choose something for me, Dominic?"

"What do you like? Are you a vegetarian? Point me in the right direction."

"I like shrimp," she said closing her menu and leaning over to look at Dominic's. "Is this good?" she asked, pointing to the item she had already decided she wanted.

He looked down at her and answered headily, "It's better than anything. Shall I order it for you?"

Christina nodded, leaving her arm on his shoulder for much longer than she needed to.

"What about you, Laura?" Mark asked, his voice sounded like granite scraping against tiling.

"I'll have the Mediterranean salad. You know I'm on a diet," she said decisively as she closed her menu. She was not poised enough to lean over Mark to examine his menu.

"What about drinks?" Dominic asked. "Tina?"

"Tonic water," she answered.

"That's not a drink," Dominic said, boldly putting his arm around her and resting his hand on her waist. "That's an ingredient for a drink."

"I like it," Christina said, looking up into Dominic's eyes and forcing the two of them into an intimate invisible bubble. "It's sweet," she breathed.

Dominic didn't answer her, instead, he seemed quietly intrigued by her, and when the waiter came and took their order, he ordered only tonic water for her.

When the interlude was over and Christina looked across the table at Mark he looked, wonderfully, annoyed beyond description. Both he and Laura looked unwell, but Christina couldn't make herself feel downhearted about it. She had never been the prettiest girl on a group date before. She had always been the tomboy, tag-along, third-wheel type. To be the one that both the men were admiring was a new experience for her. Mark clearly had eyes only for her, and Dominic was making his territory known because his arm didn't leave her waist until the food came. It was unkind, but Christina was happy. She had never seen a man get jealous or be angry because of her before. Cheers to new experiences!

When their food came, Christina thought for sure Dominic would send his steak back to the kitchen. It didn't even look like it had been cooked. When his knife bit into it, his plate practically filled with blood. Was he going to put something that raw in his mouth?

He chuckled when he saw her face and offered, "Would you like to try some?"

Laura laughed outright at Christina's screwed up nose and horrified expression. "You should try some." The other woman laughed. "You're so fond of 'enjoying the moment!'"

Christina pretended she didn't hear the dig while Dominic took a slice of the steak and put it on the tip of his fork.

Crap! Christina thought. *I only know one way out of this.* She took his fork and as she was about to place that red, raw meat into her mouth, she flipped it around and fed it to Dominic instead, allowing her hand to rest on the back of his neck.

"You're very kind," he said when he finished chewing. "Are you sure you don't want to try it?"

"I plead guilty. It's too red for me. Tonight, a girl like me can only taste sugar and spice. Blood isn't on the menu, but," she said, twisting her hair between her fingers, "I don't mind if you drink it." She looked alluring, but in her heart, she was questioning what was on his mind eating something that raw. It was disgusting.

Mark was doing his best to ignore them as he began sawing into the loaf of courtesy bread.

"Are you all right?" Laura asked him, taking the knife from him and doing it more delicately than he was able to. "Let me do that," she said.

"You're very capable," he said turning away from her and looking at the other diners instead of Laura.

Guys had said things like that to Christina many times, and she'd always taken it as a compliment. At that moment, she realized Mark meant it as an insult. Had all those boys who had said similar things to her meant to insult her? Most of them hadn't hung around. But one thing was clear, Mark didn't care if Laura was good at slicing bread or not.

Christina picked up her fork and started in on her meal. Thank goodness it was completely delicious.

***

After dinner, they went to a local movie theater. Christina fought to remember afterward which movie they saw, but it never came to her. She had spent the whole movie in the dark holding Dominic's hands in decent locations. She didn't know if he would stray, but she didn't trust him enough to take the chance. In the dark of the movie theater, she sat between Dominic and Laura, by Dominic's design. Christina thought he was trying to rub Christina's beauty in his sister's face and also keep his date as far away from Mark as possible.

After the film, the three of them went out for hot chocolate at a nearby cafe and Dominic and Laura criticized the movie for a solid hour. Christina had nothing to contribute. She hadn't been paying attention. Mark simply stared at the floor. Anytime Christina looked at him, he seemed fascinated by something away from their table.

Dominic and Christina said goodbye close to midnight on the street outside the cafe. They had already shaken off Mark and Laura.

"Do I get a kiss?" Dominic asked, moving in to get one anyway.

Christina put her fingers over her mouth and said, "That's not part of our contract tonight. Besides, you don't even want to kiss me. You were just relishing making Mark and Laura suffer."

"And you helped me!" he said positively, drawing her into an embrace. "The first time I saw you, I knew you were a good sport."

"Don't kid yourself," Christina said sharply. She didn't feel under any obligation to remain under the pretense they were on a happy date when they were alone. "It's in my contract to play your game. I keep my promises."

Dominic laughed. "Tell me you didn't enjoy teasing them?"

Christina averted her eyes. She had found some of it interesting.

"Where did you get the idea to do something like this anyway?" she asked instead of answering his question.

"My sister wants Mark. I took you away from him so he would go out with her tonight," he said.

"Forgive me if I'm wrong, but it doesn't seem to me that you like your sister very much. Why do her such a grand favor?"

"I owe her," he said simply. "Now how about if I make you a deal?"

"What kind of deal?"

"Anytime Mark phones your agency and asks for you to 'accompany' him, please promise to telephone me. I'll double whatever he offers for the night, and you won't have to bother with anything as silly as a date with me. What do you say?"

Christina frowned. She needed the money so badly, and who was Mark to her? After Valentine's Day, he would probably never think of her again without simultaneously thinking a curse. There wasn't anything there to fight for. Most likely, he hated her. Finally, she answered Dominic humorlessly, "I hope he calls every night this week."

"That's a good girl," Dominic said brightly, before helping her into a taxi.

Chapter Three

Working Nine to Five

Christina got on the bus and took a seat near the front. She pulled out her iPhone and put her headphones in her ears. She could finally afford a cell phone plan.

It was April and she had just finished her last accounting exam. It was nice to have it off her shoulders. Her course at the college had been in administrative assistance. Now it was finished, she could go look for a real job instead of escorting guys. Christina wasn't sure, but she thought the punk band in her headphones sounded like the hallelujah chorus.

As a bonus, there was one other reason she was excited about quitting her job as an escort. Once she had her evenings free again, she could maybe try to find a real boyfriend. She'd given up thinking there was a way for things to work out between her and Mark. It had been two months since Valentine's Day and he hadn't made a request for her since then. Christina kept telling herself it didn't matter. She had paid off Mindy, the college, and the credit card people as she'd planned. She was walking into the world with zero debt. All she had to do in March and April was keep 'regular Christina' away from guys and she was always fresh for work (which had been easy because she didn't normally have to beat off the guys anyway). Christina thought the price had been very low until she thought of Mark and then she wondered if it had been too high. Since it was all over, she planned to put the idea of Mark behind her. She couldn't help what had happened with him and she wanted to find herself a boyfriend. All the recent dating had left her somewhat experienced and given her a clear idea of what she *didn't* want in a guy.

Most of her escort dates were really impressed by the facade Christina and Mindy put together. They thought she was cute as a button but was that important? A guy who was impressed with a solid rack (inserts), thick eyelashes (fakes), long luscious hair (wig), and everything else that went into creating the illusion of Tina… was a guy that was simply not for her. She found herself sympathizing with Laura. Christina thought her real personality was probably more like Laura's than Tina's. She wanted a guy who saw her as a person without all that excess, added, flare. The only thing that put Christina down was her suspicion that Tina was about a zillion times more likely to score Mr. Right than Christina herself was. Well, she'd worry about that when she found Mr. Right. Until then, she'd be herself—fully and completely—and maybe he would see her. Right? She kept her fingers crossed.

Over the next few weeks, Christina kept on working at the escort service. She wasn't the only college graduate desperately trying to land herself a job. The competition was fierce, and Christina didn't have anything special to recommend her, except a stunning recommendation from the pub she had stopped working at after Valentine's Day. She had a few interviews, but nothing to get excited over.

Finally, she got an interview at Capier Incorporated. It was a job working as an assistant to a public relations officer. The lady who interviewed her was very sweet and she explained the job to Christina very thoroughly, but Christina was too excited to be there to do anything more than nod and promise she could do anything. She didn't hear a word the woman said. When Christina looked back on it, it seemed like the lights in the room were so bright she couldn't even see the woman's face.

After Christina accepted the job, she went into her jewelry box and pulled out the glasses she hardly ever wore. Clearly, she needed them if she hadn't been able to see the woman's face. Christina would need to be able to greet her when she showed up at work Monday morning.

***

When Christina got to work on her first day she suddenly realized she had been interviewed in the Human Resources department and not on the floor she would be working. She was supposed to go to room 512 on the fifth floor.

All in all, Christina felt pretty chipper. She was wearing navy trousers and a white collared shirt with a baby blue sweater-vest over-top. She had gotten her hair cut again on Saturday. Mindy had done it as a courtesy because she couldn't stand the idea of Christina going to a salon for something she considered to be little more than a buzz cut. Mindy never wore a wig herself. Her roan tresses were real. Mindy was a really good cousin to take such good care of Christina, even if she were snobby about her hair. She even got up that morning to make sure Christina sparkled for her first day at her real job.

Christina got off the elevator on the fifth floor and looked for room 512. The outer ring of the tower was lined in private offices while columns of cubicles filled the inside tracks. There wasn't even a bullpen. Pretty spiffy!

Christina found room 512. It couldn't be her office, she would probably get a cubicle, but there was her boss's nameplate. So cute! It read: Mark Lewis, Public Relations Officer.

Her jaw dropped.

She was doomed! And she thought Valentine's Day had been rough. That had literally been dinner and a movie. The next ten seconds were going to be the dictionary definition of doom.

Did the woman who interviewed her say she would be working for Mark? Christina seemed to be under the impression she would be working for the woman who interviewed her. Unless, by some miracle, that woman gave Christina the wrong room number over the phone, Christina bet that woman worked for Human Resources and was simply interviewing for Mark's assistant in his stead.

Christina stared at the door and thought rapidly. Had he seen the applications? Did he select her application because he knew she was the girl from the escort service? Christina bit her lip as heat came off her in waves. Maybe he was in his office and she should knock.

Christina raised her fist to knock when Mark himself came around the corner.

"Oh hello," he said cheerfully. "Are you Christina Witten?"

Christina smiled and put out her hand to shake his. Hers was suddenly sweaty. She hoped desperately that he wouldn't notice. The inside of his palm was like warm silk.

He shook her hand warmly and reached into his pocket to get the keys to his office. "I'm Mark. I'm sorry I wasn't there for your interview, but I was extremely impressed with what Elizabeth told me about you. It's so rare to find someone who doesn't mind working overtime—evenings and weekends. Working in PR is very exciting, but it's hard to find someone who wants to dedicate themselves to the proper representation of a company. I hope you're up to the challenge."

She had agreed to work evenings and weekends? What else had she promised?

"I am!" Christina claimed energetically. Once again, she was blindly agreeing to things, but more importantly, she wasn't certain he recognized her. Her hair was completely different, she was sans inserts, without flashy jewelry, and to ice the cake – she was wearing thick-rimmed glasses! If he didn't know she was the same person, she promised herself he would *never find out*. She clenched her fists in determination like she was about to beat the crap out of him.

He unlocked the door and invited her into his office. It was an absolute disaster. There were sliding piles of paper everywhere.

"Is this what they call 'organized chaos?'" she asked, taking a stack of paper off one of the chairs. Every surface was covered in paper.

"No," he said, sitting down at the desk and unlocking the drawers. "This is what they call 'a mess.' I don't mean to depress you, but before you do anything else, I need you to sort through this trash and file it."

Christina gulped. It was certainly going to be a great task.

"But right now we have to do something much more important," Mark said. Surprisingly, he looked even more handsome than she remembered. Maybe it was the sun coming through the blinds hitting his cheek, or maybe it was simply because he was gorgeous. He was wearing a black button-up-the-front shirt—far from formal, which she had always seen him in before. Christina thought he looked better casual. If she kept her job she was going to be in major trouble if she couldn't stop drooling over him.

"I didn't get the chance to interview you," he said. "So if you don't mind, I'd like to ask you a few questions. Would you humor me?"

"Of course," Christina said, smiling and trying to act relaxed.

"You just graduated from community college this spring?"

"Yes," Christina answered.

"And you were working at The Backhanded Pub and Grill until February?"

"Yes."

"Why did you leave that job? Your reason wasn't listed on your resume," Mark asked, leaning forward from behind his desk.

The real reason was that she could make much more money working at the escort service, but she hadn't listed her work as 'Tina' on her resume. She was worried it might damage her chances for an honest job, but then again, maybe the people working in public relations would have thought it was an asset. Christina smiled on the outside, but she cringed on the inside. Since she wasn't certain, she was going to have to lie. "I was afraid my job was interfering with my studies and I wanted my grades to be high," she answered.

"Really?" he exclaimed. "How studious! That's interesting because when I called your reference there, he said you left because you were offered a higher paying job."

Christina frowned. She couldn't believe she was caught in her lie already. "That's what I told him," she stammered. "The truth is that I was going to go work with my cousin at her place of work, but that fell through."

"So, why didn't you go back to the pub? It sounds like they would have rehired you," Mark said generously.

"Like I said, I found it was interfering—with my studies. I liked having the extra time in the evening," she answered, trying desperately to make herself sound legitimate.

"Well then, are you from the city? Did you grow up here?" he asked, allowing her slip-up to pass.

Christina answered that she grew up in a small town. She moved to the city to room with her cousin and to attend college.

"And you're only eighteen?" he asked mildly, looking at her like she was a child. That rankled her. He hadn't looked at her like that when she was Tina. He appreciated Tina as a woman, but as he examined Christina across the desk he looked like he thought she was barely out of diapers.

"No, I'm nineteen," Christina answered, her cheeks burning with fire.

"You'll learn a lot here," he said positively. "If you work hard with me, you'll probably have a fantastic job waiting for you when you're done here. Let me show you your office."

Christina noticed he didn't use the word 'cubical,' even though that was clearly where she was going to be. It was sort of sweet of him.

"You'll be stuck with me all day, so if you want a cup of coffee or anything, now's the time to say," Mark said, getting up and beckoning her to follow him to the kitchen.

"I don't drink coffee," she told him.

"That's fine. If you drink orange juice, I'll treat you today," he offered.

"Thank you," Christina said. She was following him down the hall, trying to keep up with his long strides.

***

By the end of the day, Christina had learned all kinds of things about Mark. First, he gave her a tour of the office. He showed her where the photocopier was and how to fix it when it jammed. It seemed that everyone called him before they called the repairman. Then he introduced her to the receptionist and the rest of the staff. All the women seemed to sparkle when he stuck his head into their offices. Finally, Christina reached her conclusion about him.

He was a gem! He had to be an absolute gem! Not only did he not recognize her from before, but he was honestly happy to have her working for him. He said he'd been working his job for the past seven months and he'd been promised an assistant when he was hired. But it was only recently the budget was approved for him to finally get one. He was delighted.

"Now my office will be clean," he said jubilantly. "And that's so important in our line of work. I have to invite people into my office all the time and it's so painful when it's a mess, but I don't have time to clean it."

Christina's first day of work was incredible. Working for Mark was going to be awesome!

And he'd never find out she was Tina. If she had to protect her secret to her grave, she'd do it, because as soon as he found out, she'd probably have to leave. It would be a pity. The job had been too hard to get to simply cast it off because she used to be an escort Mark hired once.

Knuckles to nose, he'd never find out.

***

When Christina got home, she told Mindy about her first day at the office and how her boss happened to be the guy who had lost the bid for her on Valentine's Day.

"Holy crap!" Mindy exclaimed noisily. "How the freak did that happen?"

"He wasn't the person who interviewed me. Instead, it was a woman named Elizabeth from Human Resources."

"And she didn't *say* that you'd be working for Mark Lewis?" Mindy asked, ultimately perplexed that such a screw-up had happened on her watch.

"I'm pretty sure she mentioned it during the interview, but I wasn't listening to her very carefully," Christina admitted bashfully. She hated owning up to her stupid side. "I was just so excited to be interviewed for such a great job."

"Well," Mindy said authoritatively, putting her feet up on the coffee table. "I don't believe for one second that he didn't know you would be the same girl. He probably watched you come in for the interview even if he didn't speak to you himself."

"But I look totally different... and men are stupid. He wouldn't have known the difference," Christina persisted.

"Even so, if he figures it out, or it comes out in the open, there's only one thing to do," Mindy said darkly. Christina wasn't sure, but sometimes Mindy acted like a gangster when it came to stuff to do with the agency.

"What's that?" Christina asked, almost jumping backward at her cousin's forcefulness. "We aren't going to kill him, are we?"

"Hmm... You just leave it to me. I'll take care of you," she said, pounding on her chest with her fist.

Chapter Four

Another Job

Christina's first week at work was a blast. She had no idea dull work could be fun if you were working with the right people. She'd often heard Mindy say things like that. It didn't matter what your job was, as long as you got to work with fun people. Well, Mr. Mark Lewis had the market cornered on making the workplace fun.

For one thing, he was absolute eye-candy. There wasn't a woman who didn't look on him like he was the 'golden boy' of the office. He was charming, charismatic, and he looked positively mouthwatering regardless of the circumstances. And Christina was his partner in crime. She was the little person he took everywhere with him. He took her to meetings and lunches with business partners while he fleshed out press releases and argued with talkative men about upcoming projects. He called it 'training.' It made her feel instantly popular and accepted by everyone in the office.

Mark stayed in his office and worked on his computer responding to emails while she tidied the place up. He didn't seem at all uncomfortable to have her there and didn't ask her to leave the room when he talked about sensitive matters with executives over the phone. Christina thought it was a remarkable display of trust because her nondisclosure agreement wouldn't be ready for her to sign until the end of the week.

Then Friday came. It would have been an ordinary day, except something unusual happened around lunchtime.

A tall elegant blonde swept through the elevator and made her way over to Mark's office. Christina didn't get the message herself, but she heard the receptionist buzz Mark to tell him Laura Figura was on her way to his office.

Christina heard it and attempted to hide her face. Mark might not be able to tell the difference between 'Christina' and 'Tina,' but Christina bet Laura would take one look at her and the jig would be up. She had to hide!

Christina sat at her desk with her head ducked behind her computer screen. She prayed Laura would slip into Mark's office without stopping to talk to her, but then she realized that Mark would probably introduce them. Christina got up. It wasn't a very mature way to deal with the problem, but she'd have to wait in the bathroom until Laura left. Besides, it was lunchtime. They were probably going out for lunch together and if Christina could just stay out of sight for just a few minutes she'd be in the clear.

Christina hurried around her desk, but whoops—she wasn't fast enough. Laura had already come around the corner and seen her.

Mark came out of his office.

Christina cringed. It was the end of the world. She was caught red-handed.

"Hi Laura," Mark said simply when he saw the blonde.

Christina looked at Mark and then looked at Laura. She couldn't help but wonder if they were still the couple Dominic said they were on Valentine's Day.

"Hello, Mark. How's work?" Laura chimed.

"I want you to meet my new assistant," Mark said, beckoning for Christina to join them. "This is Christina Witten. This is Laura Figura from Financial Services."

Christina was right about Laura. It took her about a micro minute to say, "Hello, Christina. Have we met before?"

Christina smiled but didn't even get one word out before Laura finished up.

"Ah, yes. You used to date my brother Dominic, didn't you? Or was it Alexander?" she asked.

"I don't think so," Christina said, preparing herself to tell a few white lies. "I haven't had a real date since high school."

"Really?" Laura said, not exactly sounding catty, but definitely like she didn't believe her. She sounded confident in her first instinct. Apparently, the 'Christina' in front of her was a person she could deal with, unlike 'Tina.' "That surprises me. You're very cute. Didn't you meet some exciting boys at the college?"

"I was in administrative assistance," Christina explained. "There weren't any guys in my program."

"Ah, I see," Laura said, smiling warmly.

"Are you two going out for lunch?" Christina asked, backing away. "I'll just get out of your hair. I'll have those letters ready for you by the time you get back, Mark." She walked away from them expressing internal gratitude that she didn't have to call him 'Mr. Lewis.'

Then she worked like a demon through her lunch hour. There was no way Laura wouldn't put the rest of the pieces together and bring it to Mark's attention, and then Christina would be fired. The only thing to do was to work her can off to prove to him she wanted this job whether she used to work as an escort or not.

In the end, Mark didn't come back from lunch, but instead, he called her and asked her to lock his office for him at the end of the day. He would see her on Monday morning. Something came up.

***

If Christina thought there was no price to be paid for taking a job at an escort service, she was wrong. Sure her parents didn't find out and make a fuss about the morality of it and the possibility of her being attacked, drugged or raped, but worrying about what Mark was going to do when he came back to the office on Monday was torture.

On Sunday morning, Mindy came into the kitchen with the cordless phone and asked, "Do you feel like doing one more job for the escort service?"

Christina sat at the breakfast table nursing a bowl of blueberry yogurt and thinking about her trouble. "One more job?" she asked emphatically. "Heck no! I'm already in deep water. I told you all about it."

"You mean how that crabby woman from Financial Services met you as Tina twice and now she's going to reveal your true identity to Mark?"

"Yeah," Christina whined. She was so depressed about the prospect of being canned from her first real job and even more depressed about losing Mark. She'd probably never get another boss like Mark. Forget boyfriend. A boyfriend you only saw for a couple of hours in the evening. Her boss was around eight hours a day.

Mindy abruptly came up and grabbed Christina by the hair. "Since when did you turn into such a friggin' sissy?"

"You're hurting me!" Christina bawled.

"Then stop being so pathetic," Mindy raged. She let go of Christina and slammed the phone on the table. "This is your chance to remove all suspicion that you and 'Tina' are actually the same person."

"How so?"

"The person who's requested you is Dominic Figura. Isn't he the guy who outbid your precious Mark on Valentine's Day?"

"Yes," Christina answered.

"Didn't he pay so much for you just so that Mark wouldn't get to have you?"

Christina nodded.

"Then, here's what I think. I think Dominic is asking you again because his snotty sister wants to show Mark that you are Tina."

"All the more reason why I shouldn't go!"

"Do you want me to grab your hair again?" Mindy threatened, towering over her. "If you don't show up, it might seem like an admission of guilt. Here's what I say you do. Dominic said he wants to take you to a charity carnival. There is no doubt in my mind that Mark and Laura will be there also. I'll dress you up in a dark wig. I'll also find you some brown contacts. You'll be Cleopatra by the time I'm finished with you and no one will dare think that you are the same person as Christina. You'll be in the clear if you can manage to trick them into believing that you're a completely different person. You can pull it off, can't you?"

Christina started to see things from Mindy's perspective during her speech. Mindy was right. She should grab the bull by the horns and deal with it.

"Okay!" Christina said, gathering up all her energy. "When is the date?"

Mindy looked at her watch. "You're supposed to meet him at the front gate at two o'clock this afternoon. It's ten now. Get in the shower," Mindy ordered, pushing her. "You'd better be out in exactly ten minutes. It's not like you have any hair to wash and that's just enough time to shave your legs. Move it!"

Christina had a shower and did everything else Mindy told her to do. Today, Mindy decided that Christina was going to wear a yellow sweater with white jeans. She would wear a heavy white belt over her sweater. To top it off,

Mindy also gave her a pair of white witch boots with wicked ten centimeter heels.

"Don't trip," she said coldly as she set them by the door for Christina.

Mindy wasn't kidding when she said she needed all four hours. She used almost every moment. By the time she was finished, Christina did indeed look like Cleopatra. Her wig was dark brown with a few gold highlights. Once she was wearing the brown contacts, she was also suddenly given license to wear twice as much eye makeup as usual. Mindy used a different color of foundation as well. Christina looked completely different.

At two o'clock, she was waiting for Dominic outside the fairgrounds. Christina had never felt as confident in her escort garb as she did that afternoon. She was so empowered. She was positive she made the people standing within a fifteen-foot radius feel the vibe.

Then all at once, Dominic, Laura, and Mark appeared near the entrance. She waved to Dominic and he approached her.

"Is that you, Tina?" he asked *after* she kissed his cheek.

"Yeah, of course. What is it? You look surprised," she said, taking off her sunglasses and looking at him roguishly.

"You just look totally different from before," he said.

"I was blonde on Valentine's Day, wasn't I?" she flirted, not daring to look at Mark and Laura. She didn't understand why Mark played Dominic's game. Wasn't he better than Dominic? Wasn't he brave enough to ask her directly? And not only that, but it really looked like Dominic hadn't lied when he said that Mark and Laura were dating. They had to be a couple, since they were still together, right?

"Don't women usually go darker in the winter and lighter in the summer?" Dominic asked coyly.

Yeah, he would be the type of guy who knew that. Blah... he probably even read chick magazines. Christina wanted to shoot herself. Somehow in the rush of preparation, she had forgotten he was the devil.

"Normally," she said, still not losing the gleam of trouble in her eye. "But I didn't want your sister to think that you'd stopped dating 'thrilling' women," Christina said before she turned around and greeted Mark and Laura. "Laura! Darling, you look wonderful. That diet of yours is a miracle worker. You look simply radiant." Then she took Mark's hand and shook it, trying her best to make her handshake feel different from 'Christina's.' "It's nice to see you again," she said to Mark, right before she turned around and poured all her attention on Dominic again. "One hundred dollars an hour," was what she whispered to herself as she took his arm.

Dominic didn't seem like his ordinary tricky self as he took her around the carnival. They went past a petting zoo and a merry-go-round, but he didn't seem interested in anything until they got to the games where you got to shoot things. Mark stood beside him and they both shot twenty rounds at paper targets. Christina half expected one of them to be a good shot, but both of them hit nothing but air.

Afterward, Dominic said to Mark and Laura, "I'm going to take Tina to get something to eat. Why don't you both go... pet some goats or something?" He didn't even wait for their answer before he put his hand over Christina's and headed toward one of the hotdog carts.

"Are you really that anxious to lose them?" Christina asked as she turned into the heartless wench she had transformed into the last time they were alone.

"You didn't call," he said sourly.

"Mark never called and made a request for me," Christina said sternly. "I thought that was the deal. Besides, I don't phone clients and ask them to take me out."

"Why not?" he demanded.

"I'm here for you—for your needs. I don't have needs when I go on a date with you. I am here for your comfort and pleasure only. I do not phone and ask to fulfill your needs. You call me. Even you should understand that much about all this."

"Well, I thought I did. I'm probably just being an idiot, but going out with you is a lot different than dating the girls I know," he said, slipping his sunglasses over his rogue eyes. "You're not afraid to show affection in public. You aim to make others jealous. I never saw a girl do that before. Even today."

"That's because that's what you want," Christina said. "I'm good at reading people."

"Then you're the only person who's good at reading me."

"You can't think of me that way," Christina said as he steered her away from the food carts and toward the grassy park.

"The thing is, I want to take you on a real date; get to know you and you get to know me. If it's money you want, I understand that a woman has to make her living somehow. I'm really well off, I could give you a bank account with plenty of money. If you'll give yourself the chance to get to know me," Dominic said.

Christina couldn't believe he said that. It had to be a trick. Mark and Laura were probably waiting in the bushes somewhere watching to see what would happen next.

"I don't believe you. If you really wanted that with me, then you would have called me sooner. It's June now, Dominic. Our last date was in February," she said coldly.

"I didn't realize I felt this way until I saw you standing there with your dark hair. Blondes never did turn me on," he said, moving to touch her hair.

She slapped his hand away. If he touched her hair, he would feel it was a wig. "Like I'm going to fall for a cheap line like that! Exactly who do you think you're talking to? Some country kid who just climbed out of the pumpkin patch?"

"You're too good," he said, contorting his mouth into something that almost looked like a smile.

Christina let go of his hand and pulled his sunglasses off his face. "Another thing is that a man who was truly sincere wouldn't confess while wearing sunglasses. Nothing you do strikes me as the actions of a man who's truly in love or even interested. You're playing another warped little game with your sister and her boyfriend, aren't you?"

"That's what I thought before I saw you today," he said wickedly. "Unfortunately, I have to pay off my sister before I can play the games I like. So for now, we're playing her game and I paid you to play it," he said, grabbing both Christina's arms and pulling her close to him so that their noses almost touched.

"Okay, so tell me what you want me to do. I'm on your side."

"You see Mark, over there. I need you to do something to make him change his mind about you. My sister wants to marry him, but he won't consent because he says he can't get you out of his mind and he hates the idea of being in love with someone as false as you. So, his attraction for you is keeping him from my sister—even though he doesn't want to be with you either. Think you can do something about that?"

Christina was puzzled. "So you wanted me to come today looking... unattractive?"

"What? Women are insane. You look different today, but you're so damn flirty that it doesn't matter if you're flirting with me, or him. He probably still admires you. I need you to cross the line and—"

"Make out with you?" Christina finished for him. "I'm not doing that. But if it would make you feel better, I'll go breakup with him. I'll go tell him to forget about me. It might take him a bit longer, but then he might decide to marry your sister after all."

"You'd go that far?" Dominic asked his eyes narrowed.

"Of course," Christina said, pushing his hands off her and moving away. "Do you think I want our little game to ruin his real life? How stupid. Besides, both of you are forgetting something really important."

"Which is?" Dominic asked.

"I have a life outside this," Christina said over her shoulder as she walked away to find Mark.

***

Mark and Laura were eating outside one of the hotdog stands. Christina walked up to them—a total of ten centimeters taller than she was normally—and asked Mark if she could talk to him privately.

Laura looked vexed by that little development but allowed Mark to go without kicking up much of a fuss.

Christina walked with him out of the fairgrounds and to the parking lot. She had no plans to go back to Dominic afterward. She will have fulfilled her obligation to him by then. Besides, Laura had definitely figured out she was Tina—or Laura was an idiot. She had probably already told Mark the truth about her and Christina was just screwing herself over trying to avoid the truth.

"Mark," Christina said, leaning against the carnival sign. "I hear that Laura wants to marry you."

Mark looked confused. "Why do you want to talk to me about that?"

"Well, Dominic told me. He's a devil and a half, isn't he?"

"Yeah," Mark said, turning away.

"I need to talk to tell you something important, but first I want to confirm something with you. Dominic told me that you really like me and that's why you won't marry her."

Mark took a deep breath. "Sorry about that," he said. "I was using you as a scapegoat. You have nothing to do with it. I was just using your name as an excuse because I thought I'd never see you again. I don't want to marry her or even date her, but she won't give up on me. If you were around to get caught up in this mess, I would have made up a different story. If that makes any sense." He paused. "I owe you an apology. I didn't mean to pull you into something like this."

Christina smiled. "That's a relief, but I sort of have another problem I'd like to talk to you about if I could."

Mark didn't say anything. He looked grim. Maybe it was just because Christina said it was a relief that he didn't like her. Christina thought that it must have been her imagination, but didn't he usually laugh at difficulties when they were at work?

"You see," Christina began. "I sort of had some trouble last summer. I was planning on going to college, but I missed the deadline for a grant and for a scholarship. My student loan and savings weren't enough to pay for my second semester or my housing. I was in a lot of trouble and the last thing in the world I wanted was to go home with my tail between my legs. So, I ended up taking a job at an escort service to pay my tuition and my living expenses."

"Naturally," Mark said, looking like he was bored and wanted to go.

But Christina was going to make him listen to all of it. "After graduation, I got that job working as your assistant."

Mark's eyes bugged out of his head. "You mean, Laura was telling the truth?"

"Yeah," Christina admitted.

"I didn't believe her."

"No, my cousin takes good care of me. She helps me look like this. The thing is, I'm really the girl that works in your office. That's my true personality. I'm not like this at all. I worked for the escort service for the money. In fact, I have already quit, but I didn't want to run away from the consequences of what I did. I wanted to face you honestly and tell you I don't want to be an escort anymore. I want to be your assistant quite badly. Please don't can me over this."

Mark stepped away from her. "I don't think I can use this as grounds to sack you, but it could turn into a scandal. It would be especially bad if Laura reports us, and I wouldn't put it past her."

Christina stared. She had never thought there would be consequences for the company.

"But *I* might get off the hook since you didn't disclose that you were an escort on your resume," he continued. "Also *I* didn't hire you personally."

"You mean you're thinking about your own hide?" she asked.

"Why would I worry about you?" he asked boldly. "You're not going to suffer from this, and actually neither am I. The only thing that's going to suffer is our *company's name and discretion.*"

The sound of his voice when he said those four words made Christina's blood ignite—she thought she would explode. "You are so full of crap. You may not have hired me as your assistant in the company, which yes, is a shield you can use to cover your tracks if you like, saying you didn't know who I was when I was hired. But you did hire me personally to escort you to that party. You hired me!" she yelled.

"What if the press gets involved?" he questioned angrily.

"Oh, poor Mark," she pouted. "Who do you think you are? You're not the C.E.O. or a vice president. You're not even the director of our division. You're just a P.R. officer who couldn't get an assistant. No one cares about your dirty little secrets. You are not important enough to warrant a scandal. The worst thing that could happen is your boss will call you into his office and talk to you about it seriously, and then laugh. That's right. I think he'll laugh."

That seemed to take Mark down a notch. His shoulders sagged and his face turned beet-red. "What do you know?"

She shook her head. "Of course, I will take responsibility for what I did. Oh golly, I went on one date with you and so now I'm blacklisted for life. Dang!" She paused for a second before she started in again. "And you, Mr. Lewis, think you're so friggin' cute and you know what? You are. So cute that it nearly broke my country-girl heart when you didn't outbid Dominic on Valentine's Day. I needed the money badly that night and I hadn't worked since New Year's. But if you had called me any other night of the week, I would have said 'yes' and gone with you for free. You know, I didn't want to be an escort. It's not my style! I'm not even sexy without Mindy's help, but I needed to eat. That's right! Things had been going so badly I had to skip meals—often. Perhaps you didn't notice the way I inhaled my meal on Valentine's—"

"I noticed," Mark said quietly, interrupting. "I noticed. I just didn't think it was anything that serious."

Christina stopped talking and stood there panting for an instant. She needed to catch her breath.

Mark suddenly put a hand over his eyes and said, "Look, Christina, this has been a lot to take in. You're right. I think I exaggerated how serious this was. I'll talk to my boss tomorrow morning and see what he thinks is best. Why don't you go home now and I'll explain your absence to Dominic? If he doesn't want to pay you for the whole time because you ducked out early, I'll cover your fees."

"Thanks," she said, turning around and calling Mindy to ask her for a ride. She couldn't think of a good reason to bother with a taxi now that her alias was shot.

Chapter Five

Monday Morning

On Monday morning, Christina got dressed with unusual deliberation. She intentionally dressed herself to look prudish. She couldn't help it. If she showed up at work looking even a little bit playful she knew it was going to be a day of backlash. She wore black trousers, a white collared shirt, no accessories, and only minimal product so that her short hair didn't look unruly. Her glasses looked thick even after she applied her mascara. She had to look professional and steady.

When she came into the office, Mark was waiting for her. Leaning against the wall in the reception area, he said, "Drop your bag off at your desk. We have a meeting with Collin this morning." Then he handed her his half-filled coffee mug and said, "Oh, and please top me off."

Christina took the mug from him and headed down the hallway toward her desk.

Collin? Christina had heard the name before from one of the other girls in the office, but what had she said about him? Christina flipped through her office directory until she found him, but it wasn't easy since Mark hadn't told her his last name and that was how the names were alphabetized. His name was Collin Jackson and he was the director in charge of marketing and public relations. He was Mark's boss. The thought made her shoulders slump. They had to explain their mess to someone *that* important. Ugh!

Christina dragged herself to the kitchenette and tossed out Mark's coffee so she could pour him a new cup. If only she could remember what she heard about Collin. She knew it would make all the difference, but nothing came to mind as she walked back to reception. She took a deep breath and handed Mark his coffee.

She wasn't sure if Mark was as rattled as she was. He looked almost the same as always, except that he was wearing a suit and tie instead of his usual black attire. Maybe he paid a little extra attention to what he wore that morning the same way she had. That thought was sobering for Christina. After all, he was only twenty-four or twenty-five, and still starting in the professional world in the same way she was. He was just as worried about his future as she was about hers. She ought to be easier on him. Although, she couldn't wish she hadn't yelled at him. She honestly felt everything she said was correct and he was just being arrogant.

Mark looked at the clock. It was a quarter after nine. "Okay, time to go. Are you ready?" Mark asked her skeptically.

"Yes," she said, even though she was very nervous. Normally, when she went to a meeting, she took a notebook with her, but of course, there would be nothing to jot down. It made her feel like she was going to her last meeting.

Mark took her up the elevator to the next floor. "Collin lives with the marketing people instead of with the P.R. officers. They need more room when they prepare for their advertising campaigns, so the biggest offices are up there."

The marketing floor was much different than the offices Christina was used to. There were tables laid out for design and there were tons of old posters and campaign material everywhere. The people working there also looked a lot different. They seemed to Christina to either be very chic or very... non-chic. In other words, she saw a woman dressed as a goth consulting a man in a green plaid shirt. No one in the place was dressed like Mark and Christina. They looked like high powered executives compared.

After speaking with the receptionist, Mark steered Christina into the corner. Collin's office was not at all what she expected a director's office to look like.

While it was a warm, sunny June morning, all the blinds in Collin's office were pulled tightly shut. Instead, track lights gave all the illumination that was necessary to stop the place from being completely like a bedroom. His office was large enough for a couch and actually, there were two. Both of them were covered in zebra print furry blankets. It was really the director's office? How strange. But at the same time, Christina wanted to laugh. She suddenly remembered what she heard about Collin. The other office girls said he was a complete womanizer, but a lovable womanizer. He was the center of the office gossip. He had to have a girlfriend. She had to be someone who worked for Capier, but who was she?

Christina inwardly chuckled. Mark had to explain their situation to a man who had his office decorated like the inside of a party van? Yeah. Christina had been right. There was no way he was going to hit the roof.

However, even though Christina felt relieved, the problem was still not resolved. If she couldn't get along with Mark (her real boss) on a day-to-day basis, she might as well find a new job. It looked like he was still mad at her.

Mark knocked politely on the door-frame since the door was wide open and a melancholy voice called from within, "Mark, is that you?"

"Yep!" Mark said cheerfully, sounding every inch the 'go-getter.'

They went in and Christina got a chance to look at Collin. He was a piece of work—dark with deep hollows in his cheeks and a ridge in his chin. He sat in his swivel chair like it was a throne covering his eyes with one hand and tossing the other hand carelessly aside. He held a pair of glasses in that hand as he beckoned for them to sit down.

"Ah, Mark," Collin said, taking his hand away from his brown eyes. "What have you done now?"

"Do you mind if we close the door?" Mark asked.

Collin rested his scruffy chin on his bony knuckles and agreed.

"Christina, would you mind?" Mark asked.

Christina immediately got up and closed the door for them, making the room even darker and more intimate since the light from the hall was gone. Mark didn't speak again until Christina joined him on the couch.

"Do you remember a conversation we had last winter before the seasonal office party?" Mark asked.

Collin looked at Mark like his opening statement was the last thing he expected to hear. "Sorry, I don't. Around Christmas last year, the only thing I remember was fighting with the board of directors that Internal Relations shouldn't be part of my division. As if I can handle office drama as well as our corporate image. How stupid!"

"I remember the restructuring hassle," Mark said steadily. Christina kept her tongue in her head as he proceeded with his voice that was smoother than butter. "But what I was talking about was our conversation before the New Year's party. You asked me if I had a date, and when I admitted I hadn't had time to ask anyone, you suggested I call an escort service."

Christina nearly choked. His boss had been the one who told him to call for her? What the heck had Mark been going on about consequences the day before?

Collin laughed. "Yeah. I remember. So? Why's this coming up now?"

Mark didn't stutter or choke or anything, he just said, "Well, I decided to take your advice."

"You did?" Collin laughed. "I think I saw who you brought. She was stunning. So, how did it go? But, Mark, I have to ask you. It's great that you're telling me this—I'm really interested—but I would have been more interested in January. Why is this coming up now? And why did you bring your assistant? You could have just walked in."

"She needs to be here. You see here, my new assistant, Christina Witten. She is the escort I hired that night," Mark said, introducing her.

Collin's eyes bugged out of his head.

"You have to understand I didn't hire her as my assistant myself," Mark started. "Elizabeth from Human Resources took care of it for me. Also, when I knew Christina as an escort, she went by the name 'Tina.' When she came to work for me as my personal assistant—I didn't recognize her. However, Laura *did* recognize her and informed me. I didn't believe her, but then Christina told me herself that was the case."

"Really?" Collin said, looking speculative. "Really? Hmm…"

Christina bit her lip. There, Mark had got the chance to explain himself to his boss, so everything should be square with them, right?

Suddenly, Collin got up from his chair and came over to where Christina and Mark were sitting. "Stand up," he said.

Christina and Mark both got up.

"Not you," Collin said to Mark. "Just her." He was looking at Christina very carefully. "Christina," he said mildly. "Would you mind standing under one of my track lights for a second?"

"Not at all," Christina stammered as she moved to stand where he told her to.

"Would you take off your glasses, please?"

She took them off.

Then Collin asked, "Are your eyes are naturally green?"

"Yes."

He was looking at her face very closely. It was making her so uncomfortable she started sweating.

"I'm not sure what you're looking for," Christina asked, looking over Collin's shoulder at Mark.

Mark was shaking his head and pacing.

"Do you have a complicated morning routine for your skin?" Collin asked suddenly.

"No. Why?"

"Because, it's damn near perfect," he said moving away from her. "You had long hair at New Year's, didn't you? Have you had a haircut since then?"

"Not exactly," Christina answered. "I normally wear my hair shorter than this. I was wearing a wig."

"And did you always wear a wig when you dressed up as an escort?" Collin went on.

"Always, but I don't work for the agency anymore."

"Did you do your hair and makeup yourself for these occasions or do you have someone at your agency help you?"

"My cousin Mindy used to help me. Why?"

"Well, you see, I had heard of an escort called 'Tina' before today," Collin said, picking up his coffee cup and sipping from it.

"What?" Christina stammered, but not as quickly as Mark.

"You've heard of her before?" Mark piped up.

"Last night I was talking to a friend of mine about the new ad campaign we want to introduce for the fall, advertising one of our cell phone lines. For ages we've only used one model," Collin explained as he pulled out a black and white poster of the ad from last year.

Christina unrolled it and saw one of the most beautiful men she'd ever seen. It was a perfect picture of his profile as he stood on a corner of a busy city street. The traffic was flying by him and his long pale hair was rustled by the energy of it. He had a headset in his ear and basically looked like the epitome of masculinity. Christina had seen the ad before. It always made her want to buy their brand.

"The model in that picture is Alexander Figura. Since you've met Laura you might as well know he is her half-brother."

"Really?" Christina asked, flabbergasted. She never would have thought.

"The point is," Collin continued. "We've been looking for a female model to work with him, but finding someone has been most troubling. No one is tall enough, pale enough, or flexible enough. I was talking to Dominic last night and he told me that he knew an escort called 'Tina' who would be perfect for the job."

"Dominic!"

"He's Alexander's agent," Mark explained.

All the hair on Christina's neck suddenly stood on end. Dominic had said something the day before about playing his games. Son of a gun! He wasn't going to stop.

"Anyway," Collin continued. "If you can do it, I'd like to see how you look with Alexander. As I said, we've been driving ourselves crazy looking for someone to match him and if there's a chance you would work, I need to try. Interested?" Christina didn't get to answer before Collin finished up by saying, "Even if you didn't work here, I think Dominic was planning to call your agency to set up a meeting."

"Oh!" Christina said. "So you're not worried I used to work for an escort service?"

"No," Collin said, sounding impatient. "Everyone has to start somewhere and if you don't know how to make some odious person happy then you're worthless in our line of work. Now all you have to learn is how to smooth talk like Mark and you'll be the heir of greatness. What do you say to meeting Alexander to see if we can pair you up?"

Christina's wanted a chance to think, but what Collin was asking for really wasn't much. He just wanted her to meet a ridiculously handsome man to see if she looked good beside him. She didn't want to get caught up in Dominic's garbage, but a chance to model with Alexander... should something like that be passed up just because there are one or two slimy people?

"What do you need me to do?" Christina asked.

"Just dress up like you normally do when you're going to go on a date with someone. So, if you wear a wig, wear a wig. That sort of thing," Collin said, getting back behind his computer.

"But normally, I dress up for a particular situation. Could you give me a little more guidance? I'm not an actual model. I used to work as an escort which means that 'yes' I specialized in being the pretty little trophy on a man's arm, but I need more information than which man I'm going to accompany," Christina said, feeling like she was slipping back into Tina's shoes.

Collin smiled. "Dominic was right about you. You'll work splendidly."

"What *did* Dominic say about me?"

Collin glanced at Mark.

Mark's jaw was clenched. Yeah, he looked furious. His eyes were practically on fire.

After a moment's pause, Collin answered her, "Just dress in fall colors. Last season's styles are fine. I'll tell Dominic to dress Alexander in the same thing and I'll have my assistant contact your office with the day we schedule." Christina noticed Collin successfully avoided her question. He had to know something about the situation she didn't know, or something she didn't want him to know.

After that, Mark hustled Christina out of Collin's office and hurried her downstairs. It was clear things had gone badly from his perspective and from that point on, they were only going to get worse.

***

Christina got an email from Collin's assistant the next day. He informed her they hadn't been able to nail Alexander down for a meeting until the end of the week. The meeting was on Friday afternoon at two o'clock in Collin's office.

Shortly afterward, Mark called her in to see him. He had not been himself since their meeting on Monday. He had been the 'golden boy' of the office, but in week two, he was more like the grouch who only surfaced from his trashcan to complain. Working for him the week before had been so pleasant and since the meeting, it was exactly how she always imagined work to be—a chore.

Christina closed the door (under his instructions) and sat down.

"Always close the door when we're alone in here from now on, okay?"

"Okay," she drawled slowly.

"Sorry about what I said to you at the carnival," he said. "I realized after you left you were probably right and working a more reputable job had to be your goal all along.

Otherwise, you wouldn't have tried to get a job working as one. If you liked being an escort, then why even finish college? I overreacted and everything you said put things into perspective for me. I was being pigheaded."

"Yeah, you were," Christina said easily. "But I appreciate the apology. It shows you're not really pigheaded. You just had a flare of panic. Don't worry about it."

"Thanks for that," he said. "If I could, I'd like to ask you something."

"Sure," Christina said, thinking how handsome he was when he was humble. The way his head bent down thirty degrees was absurdly cute.

"How well do you know Dominic?"

"I've only met him those few times when you were around."

"Really? It seemed to me you two must know each other much better than that if he's trying to make you a model."

"I don't know where the motivation for that is coming from. I never told him that I wanted to be a model. Modelling isn't on my to-do-in-this-lifetime list. I didn't even know what he did for a living. So, he's an agent for his brother, eh? I thought he'd do something more..."

"More?"

"Evil," Christina finished.

"You don't think being the agent of one of the highest-paid male models in our country is evil?" Mark asked dryly.

"Is it?" Christina asked innocently.

"I don't know if Alexander would be what he is today if Dominic wasn't willing to do everything he could to make sure he was a success. Dominic's very persistent, strong-willed and very rich—which is why I couldn't outbid him on Valentine's. Sorry, Christina, but if I said I was willing to pay a hundred dollars an hour for you, then Dominic would have paid two hundred an hour. I never would have been able to outbid him. My year's income doesn't touch his. Surely you noticed he paid the whole bill for dinner at that fancy restaurant on Valentine's?"

"Yeah, I noticed. I didn't think anything of it, but Mark, you suck. You should have called and said you'd pay a hundred an hour," Christina said, still thinking with her impoverished brain.

"What? Why should I have done that?"

"Because then I could have got two hundred dollars an hour from dating that blood drinker!"

"You really did it for the money!" Mark laughed, seeing dollar-signs fill her eyes. For one second, he looked like the Mark she knew the week before. He leaned back in his chair and looked content, but then a thought seemed to cross his mind and the mirth left his face. "Can I ask you a personal question about being an escort?"

"Go ahead."

"I was just wondering how detached you are when you play 'Tina.' Is the real you close to the surface or do you almost forget about your true self?"

Christina knew what he was talking about. Only a person who pretends to be something that they're not will know what it is to deny yourself natural expression. "Well, when I was first doing it, there was no difference between 'Christina' and 'Tina,' except in our appearances. We were the same and I was just putting forth the effort to make the man I was dating was comfortable. But, I think you're right, as I got further into being her, my only quality as 'Tina' was feeling the needs and preferences of the person next to me and trying to do what would make them happy."

"That's what modeling is all about," Mark said. "It's about feeling out the photographer or the director and achieving the image they want. You'll probably make a great model, even though I'm against it."

"Why would you bother being against it?"

"One other question, Christina," he said, sidestepping her. "Did you really tell all your dates you liked them?"

Christina shook her head. "Why would I do something stupid like that? It's just a game."

"What about what you told me?" he asked her, his eyes looking specifically interested.

Christina realized it was a trap. At first, she didn't know how to answer him. Was it really okay to have an office romance with your boss? Christina had always thought your boss was strictly off-limits. He was the last person in the world you should try to date. It might look like you were trying to use him to get promoted… but Mark couldn't promote her. He was new, too. All the same, she thought it was best to stay out of trouble. It didn't matter whether she liked Mark or if she went so far as to think he was the best thing she had ever seen. She couldn't get involved. "You're too handsome for me," she said flippantly, before excusing herself from his office.

"Hey! I didn't tell you to leave," Mark called after her.

So, she had to come back in, close the door, sit down like a good little girl, and pretend she hadn't just been flirting with her boss.

"On Friday, don't worry about coming in first thing in the morning," Mark said, sounding like her boss again. "Your timesheet will be the same. I was just thinking it probably takes you some time to affect your transformation into 'Tina,' so come in at two o'clock for your meeting with Alexander and then you can go home. If it's okay with you, I'd like to keep it quiet in the office the fact they're even considering you for the job of modeling for that campaign. If things go well and you're chosen, I'd like you to keep it to yourself until the last minute. I hate office gossip."

Christina nodded, seeing his point of view. She guessed 'Tina' couldn't die quite yet.

Chapter Six

Model Man

When Mindy heard the news that Christina had been invited to a trial photoshoot with Alexander Figura, she was ecstatic.

"It's all because of me!" she proclaimed happily. "It's because I'm a genius! And I get to dress you up for your meeting on Friday, don't I?"

"Of course," Christina agreed quickly. From her perspective, she had no chance of getting the job without her cousin's expertise.

"I should have gone to beauty school instead of screwing around with the escort service, don't you think?" Mindy said, crawling into one of her many makeup bags looking for supplies.

"It's not too late," Christina reminded her. "You can still go. Just work yourself through school while working at the agency."

"Right," Mindy said sarcastically.

After that conversation, Christina wished she hadn't spilled the news to Mindy so soon, because she worked Christina to the bone. If Christina wasn't working at work, she was working at home pretending to be stiff as a Barbie doll. Mindy put a poster of Alexander up on the wall in the dining room and practiced different fashions and makeup styles on Christina all evening every night of the week.

Mindy was determined Christina would be hired as the model. She nearly killed both of them coming up with the perfect style to match Alexander. She went shopping during the day while Christina was at work to find the perfect autumn outfit even though the stores weren't selling fall shades in June.

By Friday morning, Mindy had come up with the perfect thing. She dressed Christina in a brown corduroy miniskirt and a black off-the-shoulder top. Then she gave her a pair of brown suede boots and topped the look off with a sleek green scarf.

The last thing was the wig. Christina knew Mindy had been nervous about its selection. In the end, she decided on the wig that Christina had worn on Valentine's Day.

"It won't be good if Alexander is more feminine than you," Mindy said decisively. "I almost think you should go red for this, but that might be risky since this Collin guy saw you in a blonde wig. He's expecting a blonde, isn't he?"

Christina nodded. She had tried on a red wig at the agency once, just to see how it looked and she was surprised to see that it turned her peaches-and-cream complexion into strawberries-and-cream. She could never be a redhead.

Mindy drove her to work herself on the day of the audition and said she'd wait for Christina.

"Don't hang around," Christina insisted. "It's okay. I don't have any idea how long this will take and parking downtown is really expensive. Can't I just call you when I'm finished?"

"Okay," Mindy agreed. "But don't get picked up and taken out by anyone... unless your meeting goes that long. Call me right away so I can hear how things went. Okay?"

Christina agreed and moved to get out of the car.

"And wear your shades, Tina," Mindy reminded her as she dropped her off in the loading zone in front of Christina's building.

Christina slid on the glasses. It wouldn't be so bad. Mark said he would meet her in the foyer ten minutes before the interview. He'd take her straight upstairs, so she wouldn't get stalled by anyone if she happened to be recognized.

Christina pushed through the revolving door and stepped onto the marble. Mark was there, leaning against the wall by the elevators.

"You haven't got any grape gum in your mouth, have you?" he asked coyly when he saw her.

"Hi Mark," Christina said cheerfully, sliding her sunglasses off her nose. "How do I look?"

Mark looked at her carefully. Then he took her hand and spun her around so that he could have a 'proper' look at her. "I should have asked you to come earlier so that I could have taken you to out to lunch before the meeting. Then I could have scored a free date with the popular and elusive Tina."

"Don't joke," Christina said as she took her compact out of her purse to make sure Mark hadn't mussed her when he twirled her.

"Who was joking?" he said.

Christina glanced up at him. There was definitely a difference in the way Mark acted toward her when she was dressed up. When she was 'Christina' she was a child who needed to be guided by him. She wasn't exactly the competent office professional he needed her to be yet, so when they were in the office together, he was still training her. But when she was 'Tina' she was no longer his trainee, but once again the woman he could never have. And from the look in his eyes—he still wanted her.

Christina smiled in response and pressed the button for the elevator.

Once they were inside with the doors closed, Christina started to think. Her relationship with Mark couldn't be divided, he had to see her for who she truly was whether she was dressed up as 'Tina' or not. He couldn't partition the two in his brain and make her two people.

"You know, Mark," she started. "Now that you know I'm wearing a wig, doesn't it seem kind of weird that I'm wearing false hair on my head? How can I possibly still look special to you when you know how fake I am?"

Mark shrugged his shoulders. "It doesn't make a difference."

"Why not?" Christina persisted.

"I don't know. Just because you know something is a trick doesn't mean it's not dazzling. You're like a magician."

Christina gulped. What was he saying? Shouldn't he at least try to hide that he thought she looked gorgeous for the sake of their professional relationship? Instead, he was closing the distance between them so their arms touched as they stood side-by-side.

The doors began to open. "Are you ready for this?" Mark asked.

Christina rolled her eyes. "Psyched."

"Take my arm," he instructed. "I'll lead you to the meeting."

Christina slipped her fingers around his elbow and allowed him to steer her past the reception desk. He was wearing a suit again and the fabric was rough. Christina smiled. Mark was so cute. After checking in, he took her to Collin's corner.

The zebra blankets had been tucked away somewhere and all the blinds were open. Collin's office almost looked respectable as Mark and Christina came in and sat down on one of the couches. Christina thought they were early, but Dominic and Alexander had beaten them there.

Dominic sat, looking like every inch the calculating devil. He wore rouge shaded sunglasses and the neck of his shirt was open. When Christina came in, she expected him to get up and hug her or at least shake her hand. Instead, he didn't move from his position on the couch and only waved slightly with one of his hands. He acted completely indifferent even though he had been the one to set up the meeting.

Alexander seemed friendlier than his brother because he smiled broadly at Christina and Mark when they came in. Yeah, he was handsome. Christina was impressed with his style. She could tell just by glancing at him that it didn't matter what he was wearing, he was going to look fantastic. He matched everything.

After the introductions and preliminaries, Collin called Christina and Alexander to stand up together to see how well they matched.

Dominic joined Collin and looked on with interest almost as if he was partially in charge. "Since hair color is an option on Tina, do you think she would look better as a brunette?"

"No," Collin said quickly. "The thing that's special about Tina is that we can match her hair to whatever shade we want, as long as it complements Alexander's. Also, her eyes—a blue-eyed girl wouldn't have filled the bill. I still haven't discarded the idea of having everything in the photos black and white except for their eyes."

"It doesn't matter," Dominic said, looking at her and Alexander together. "Your graphics wizards don't care what color her eyes are. They'll make them the color we want."

Collin frowned and picked up his camera. "You two talk!" Collin yelled at Christina and Alexander. Then he turned to Dominic and started explaining something.

Alexander turned and looked at Christina. "So, how long have you been a model, Tina?"

"I'm not really a model," Christina said carefully.

"Really?" Alexander said, looking intrigued. "That's interesting. So, what do you do? Are you an actress or a singer?"

"No. I just graduated from college."

Alexander looked confused. "Studying fine arts? Performing arts?"

She shook her head.

"Really? No? Then who recommended you for this job? You know an ad with me is a pretty big break, even if you have already worked as a model for years."

"It was Dominic's idea," Christina answered.

"That's even weirder," Alexander said, laughing. "I wonder why he's trying to get you a job. Maybe he wants to be your manager, but that seems odd, too. He never takes on clients. I'm the only one."

"He thinks I'm talented," Christina answered. "He thinks I'm good at sensing the emotions of others and supplying them with what they want. He's not the only one. Mark thinks I'll be able to sense the wants of the photographer and give them what they're trying to capture."

"Wow!" Alexander exclaimed. "That's pretty impressive. But how did you convince those two of that? They're so different. That strikes me as…" then he stopped, right in the middle of his sentence. At that moment, it was clear to Christina that Alexander realized something and it wasn't something good.

"Did Dominic tell you anything about me?" Christina asked.

Alexander shook his head like he was shaking off a particularly bad thought. "No. He didn't say anything. But he never talks about a woman unless he's insulting her, so the fact that he didn't say anything about you is a compliment." Here, Alexander actually smiled.

Maybe Alexander thought he was telling a joke. Maybe not. Whatever his thoughts, Christina was one hundred percent convinced Alexander was telling the truth. Dominic was the type of guy who used women. Christina was growing to learn that more and more. The photoshoot was just an opportunity for him to use her. But why?

"How is Laura doing?" Christina asked breezily. "I haven't seen her since last week."

"Well, then you've seen her more recently than I have," Alexander said coyly, looking at the scarf at Christina's throat. "So, I should be the one asking you how my sister is. Was she well?"

"She seemed to be doing all right," Christina answered cautiously. Alexander definitely had a scary look on his face. He was about to do something.

"Tina, do you know why Collin asked us to talk just now?"

Christina looked at him curiously and waited for him to continue.

"It's so we can get familiar with each other—comfortable. The plan for the ad casts us in the role of lovers, so we've got to get to know each other," he said, suddenly slipping her scarf from around her neck.

Maybe it was Christina's experience as an escort, or maybe it was the intensity in Alexander's eyes which Christina knew to be false. One wolf recognizes another. The reason why Christina was mesmerized was because she'd never seen a guy pull that sort of trick on her before, or be so good at it. He looked like he was interested in her, enchanted by her, and perhaps even more. He wanted her to play along and Christina was so used to the game her bottom lip quivered.

At that instant, Collin rapidly started taking pictures.

Alexander finished the moment by bringing her scarf to his lips. He kissed it lingeringly as Collin shot off with his camera.

"That's good, Lex," Collin said, as he pulled his camera away from his face. He started reviewing the shots on his digital camera when he stopped at one of them and looked hard at it. "Hmmm… Dominic, look at this one."

Christina was impressed he wasn't already leaning over Collin's shoulder.

Dominic went up and looked at it. His eyebrows flew up in the air like leaflets caught in the wind. "That's not bad," he said, scratching his nose and keeping his tone deadpan.

"Did it turn out well?" Alexander asked, approaching the two of them. Collin showed him the picture. Alexander looked less impressed than Collin and Dominic. He even stepped back quickly to make room for Mark.

When Mark saw the picture, all the air escaped from his lungs and he visibly drooped. "That's more than I expected."

"More than I expected, too," Collin said easily. "Funny, she didn't look star-struck by Alexander when she came in the door."

"I'm not," Christina said urgently.

"Really?" Mark asked leaving space beside Collin for her to have a look at the screen.

When Christina got her first look at the picture, she was stunned. Only Alexander's back was in the picture. His hands were moving around her throat to remove her scarf. He was hardly in it. The main feature of the picture was her face. The look on her face was like the open heart of a wounded bird. She looked like she was the heroine on the last page of a romance novel where she had just spent three hundred and sixty-five pages tearing her heart to shreds over Alexander and on the last page he was confessing he had been in love with her all along.

Christina didn't know what to say. She didn't know she was capable of that much emotion. It hadn't been over-acting, had it?

"Did I go too far?" she asked Collin.

"Not at all," Collin said pursing his lips together. "Actually, it makes me feel like you might be capable of a lot more than a simple still photo. We might be able to get a commercial out of you, but let's start with the photos."

Christina swallowed hard. "Does that mean you want to hire me?" she asked huskily.

"At least for the still photos," Collin said, nodding approvingly. "You don't have an agent, do you?"

Christina was about to answer 'no' when Mark piped up. "She doesn't need an agent. I'll look out for her in the place of one."

"That's ridiculous," Dominic rebuked. "Mark's not qualified for something like this. She needs a real agent."

"Does that mean you want to take her on?" Collin snickered.

"Well, I—"

"He doesn't have time," Alexander interrupted. "He keeps telling me what a full schedule we have and we truly do. The only reason why I was able to come here today was because of the importance of our business with Capier Inc. We pushed some other things aside to make room."

"We're happy to be your valued customer, Lex," Collin said soothingly. "And I wouldn't dream of letting Dominic represent Tina. Mark will do nicely."

"Why do you get to make that decision?" Dominic asked crankily. "Shouldn't a decision like that be left up to Tina?"

Collin raised an eyebrow and gave Dominic a curious look. "It's okay. Tina doesn't mind, right?"

"Of course not," she said quickly. "That's most appropriate."

"I'm glad you think so," Collin said, setting a hand on her hair.

Dominic held his peace after that and the rest of the meeting was smooth. They took more photographs. Collin liked them. They made arrangements for the time and place of the photoshoot. Mindy was going to be happy. Not only had Christina gotten the job, but she had also got Mindy an interview. Collin wanted Mindy to do Christina's makeup.

By the time the men finished gabbing it was almost four o'clock. They left Collin in his office and Dominic, Alexander, Mark, and Christina made their way down to the foyer. Once they arrived, Christina shook Alexander's hand and told him she was really happy to have met him and she looked forward to working with him. Alexander smiled but he seemed weary. He had probably heard the same speech from at least fifty other little girls. It was just another day at work for him. Their project wasn't special.

Dominic said good-bye to Christina like she was a stranger. He didn't even turn his head for one last look at her as he left the building with Alexander. Christina couldn't figure out what was going on in his head. Was he happy he had helped her or was he honestly irked Mark was going to be her 'agent?' Well, whether he regretted it or not, she was going to model with Alexander.

"Thanks, Mark," Christina said once she could stop waving at Dominic and Alexander.

"For what?"

"For protecting me from Dominic. Does he want to be my agent? Is that what this is all about?"

"I wish I knew. Maybe it's something that simple."

"Welp, you said I could go early, so I'm going to shove off now," she said brightly, pulling her sunglasses out of her bag. "See you on Monday," she called cheerfully as she headed out.

"Wait a second," he said, grabbing her arm. "Where do you think you're going looking like that?"

"I was going to go call my cousin. She wants to hear how the meeting went. Come on! I can't hold out on her. I have to let her know Collin wants to meet her."

"But where were you planning on going after that? Do you have plans for this evening, Miss Christina?"

Christina's mouth made a perfect O, but no sound came out.

"Well?" Mark persisted.

"No," she managed.

"Well, can I take you out to dinner?"

He was asking her for a date. He was honestly asking her for a date. Was it because she was dressed up and that was unusual?

Christina frowned. "Mark," she said, suddenly stepping very close to him and slipping her fingers between the buttons on his shirt. "If I went home now and took off my wig and this outfit and came out with you looking the way I normally do at the office, would you still want that date?"

He hesitated. The moron hesitated.

"I don't think I can go on a date with you," she said, backing away from him. "Sorry. I'll see you on Monday."

"Wait," he said, grasping her upper arm and stopping her. "I don't understand. Why do you have to change?"

Christina sighed. She bet he wouldn't chase after 'Christina' like that, but he couldn't take 'no' for an answer when 'Tina' was involved. "Look, Mark. Do you remember our conversation in the elevator? This person you see in front of you isn't the real me. It isn't anything like me. It's a fabrication, a facade—nothing. It's professional bunkum. Surely, you must understand that. It's a show. I know you must put on a show when you're doing your public relations thing, so you should know exactly what I'm talking about."

"I'm not sure I do know what you're talking about," he said seriously. His black eyebrows pulled tight. "Of course it's necessary to be a little more congenial when you work, especially in P.R., but I think my personality is the same whether I'm working or relaxing."

"Well, I don't feel that way," Christina said, pulling her arm out of his reach. "I change completely when I dress this way. I become outspoken, I think about how I turn my hips so I can make the most of them, I put myself completely aside for my date's comfort, and I even think I can get men to like me who would never look at me twice otherwise."

Mark clenched his jaw and swallowed. He clearly didn't know how to answer that because it didn't make sense to him. Christina expected him to look mad, but when she looked at him carefully she saw concern for her as well.

"This job of yours has really screwed you up, hasn't it?" he said finally.

"Maybe it has," she said, breathing deeply.

"Listen, I have a better idea," Mark said closing the distance between them. "Instead of taking you out for dinner, why don't I cook you dinner instead? We can even swing by your apartment on the way there so you can break the news to your cousin. Will that suit you?"

Christina cocked her head. Events had suddenly taken a very strange turn. What exactly was he planning?

Chapter Seven

Out of the Office

When Christina got into Mark's car, she was more relaxed than she thought possible. It wasn't a fancy car, but an ordinary Toyota sedan, very much like the one her parents owned. The interior was almost the same.

She gave Mark directions to her apartment. Partway through her discourse Mark stopped her. "Couldn't you just give me the address? It seems like we're just following the number twelve bus route."

Christina shuddered. They *were* following the number twelve bus route. She wasn't very familiar with the city, even though she had lived there for almost a year, and she didn't know how to get anywhere without taking the bus. She blushed and gave him the address.

Mark changed lanes and look them onto a much faster-moving road. Apparently, they had really been going the slow way.

Finally, he parked in front of her building. "Do you want to come in?" Christina asked nervously. She had never invited a guy up to her apartment before. The idea made her all twitchy.

"That was the plan," he said, taking off his seat belt.

"Why?" she asked.

"Because I came to watch you change."

"What!" Christina exclaimed. "I am not going to let you watch me change."

"Look, Christina, I'm not trying to get a glimpse of you naked or something, but I want to watch you turn into yourself. Don't you think that will take the spell off both of us?"

Christina looked at him carefully. What he said made a great deal of sense to her. He was probably right. If he watched her take off her wig, all her other flare and then saw her in her regular clothes with only her glasses to frame her eyes then the illusion would probably be destroyed. If he didn't like her for who she truly was then it would come out right away and both of them would be spared the pain of not getting who they wanted.

"Okay," Christina said, thinking there was a possibility that after he saw the transformation he wouldn't want to make her supper anymore and would simply leave the apartment. For some reason, she couldn't let that happen. She wanted a chance to convince him that 'Christina' was a really amazing girl, so she had to have dinner with him. She absolutely had to. "But, I'd rather not do that here if that's okay. Could I just get a bag and come over to your place?"

Mark looked shocked. "I guess that would be okay."

"Kay. I'll be right back," Christina said, getting out of the car and heading into the building.

***

Mindy was ecstatic about the possibility of being Christina's makeup artist for the ad campaign.

"Yay me!" she declared happily. "Where should we go to celebrate?"

Christina bit her lip and went into her bedroom without answering. She had to pack her bag.

"What are you doing?" Mindy asked when she saw Christina fill up a backpack with clothes and shoes. "You're not doing something else I shouldn't tell your mom, are you?"

"No," Christina said, realizing full well that it looked like she was packing an overnight bag. "I'll be back tonight. I won't be fooling around or anything."

"What *will* you be doing?" Mindy asked seriously.

Christina thought about telling her what she and Mark had planned but decided against it. Mindy probably wasn't the type to sympathize with that level of understanding, and Christina didn't want to be ridiculed. She doubted Mindy ever let a man see her without war paint. "None of your business," she said, sliding her makeup remover into the bag.

"Okay, but phone if you're going to be home later than two. If I wake up in the morning and you're not here, I'll call your parents and ask them if you went home for the weekend."

Christina brushed her off. "I'm not staying out all night."

She gathered the rest of her stuff together and went down to Mark's car. She opened the backdoor and threw her bag in before she got in the front seat.

"Does it really take that much stuff?" he asked her.

"Yes, it does."

"Okay then," he said, shifting the car into reverse. "This is probably going to be a very illuminating experience for me."

***

Mark's apartment was a lot nicer than Christina expected after seeing his car. There was hardwood flooring. The countertops were marble, the appliances were sparkling stainless steel, the sofa was leather, and the plants were real.

Christina sat down on the couch and said, "You must make a lot more money than I do."

Mark shrugged his shoulders. "This isn't really my place. It's my brother's. He's just not living here right now. It's not even my style, but it's a dang sight better than living in the type of place I could afford. The biggest bonus is that I don't have to have roommates."

She nodded.

"Are you disillusioned about me?" Mark asked.

"What do you mean?"

"I haven't got a fancy car. Surely you saw the Jaguar Dominic drives. No? And this place; sure, it's nice, but it's not mine," he said dryly. It was like he was trying to pull the wool off Christina's eyes in the same way she was trying to disenchant him.

"Do you think I'm impressed with money?" she questioned.

"You could be. I can't get the way you talked about your escort service job out of my head. You really did it for the money, so I thought it was a given that you care about that sort of thing."

"I only took that job because I was practically starving. Come on, I told you before I don't harbor any little dreams of becoming a model or an actress. I want to be an administrative assistant and build off that. I don't want to live a glamorous life and live continuously in the spotlight." She paused. "Actually, this place is kind of intimidating. You need to know that my kitchen has lino flooring and the fridge and the stove are different colors? We don't even own a dishwasher."

"But doesn't that make you aim for something better?" Mark asked as he sat down on one of the arms of the sofa.

"No. Actually, I didn't realize how mismatched my apartment was until I saw your arrangement. Most of the stuff in my apartment isn't even mine. It belongs to my cousin. So, you and I are in a similar situation. You just have a wealthier relative," she said with a smile. "Besides, I think

I'm even more comfortable with you knowing that this stuff isn't yours. This is a pretty sterile place, isn't it?"

Mark smiled and moved to a chair exactly adjacent to where Christina was sitting.

"Now it's your turn," he said. "I've shown you mine. You show me yours."

Christina bit her lip. He was right. For men, it often seemed like their appeal was based on their purchasing power instead of themselves. She couldn't blame him for being a little nervous when she was the type of girl to sell herself for a hundred dollars an hour, which made her too expensive for his blood.

She reached into her bag and pulled out a mirror, which she propped on the coffee table between them and tilted toward her face. Then she crossed her legs and prepared to get started.

"The first thing to come off is the wig," she said pulling the claws out of her hair. Once it was off her real hair (though short) was pinned down in the front. It was terribly flattened, because wig hair was worse than hat hair. "Look at this," she said, showing Mark the inside of the wig. "These claws go into my real hair to hold the wig in place."

"Are they uncomfortable?"

"They feel okay for the first couple of hours, but I can't wear it for more than eight hours or I'll have a legendary headache. But it also depends on how heavy the wig is. This is a heavier one because of its length. The wig is the last thing I put on before I leave for a job." Christina combed it before she put it away in its bag. "Next thing to come off is all this jewelry," Christina said as she started stripping her ears of their dangling earrings. "None of this stuff belongs to me," Christina explained.

"Whose are they?" Mark asked.

"My cousin Mindy's. She's the one who got me into escorting. She owns a lot of clothes, a lot of jewelry, and a lot of makeup. She could probably start her own agency just on her personal stash. The wig is borrowed from the escort service though. Mindy has beautiful hair and would never degrade herself by wearing a wig. She's more like the real-meal-deal whereas I'm just a substitute for when she's got too many clients."

"I didn't realize you thought of yourself that way. You might be prettier than she is," Mark commented.

"I might be, but I think that depends on what you think is beautiful. So, once I've got all that crap off me, then it's time for the false eyelashes to come off," she said, getting enthusiastic.

"You wear fake eyelashes!" Mark exclaimed.

"Yup. Not only am I sort of fair; I don't have dark eyelashes, but mine aren't very long, so fake eyelashes are an absolute must." She looked extremely different once they were removed.

Christina couldn't stand to look at Mark during that phase of her transformation. It was too much. No woman likes to be wiped completely clean of all makeup in front of the guy she likes. Besides, even Christina wore eyeliner and mascara on a regular basis. Without those, her face was all the same color.

She reached into her hair and pulled out the pins. She shook her hair out and said quietly, "Now there are only the clothes left. Oh, and these," she said, reaching into her shirt and pulling her inserts out of her bra. It would be a meaningless exercise if she didn't go all the way. She dropped them on the floor between them and was aware her shirt was considerably looser.

She couldn't look at Mark. It was just too hard.

"I'm going to go change my clothes now," she said, getting up and grabbing her bag. She disappeared around the corner and found the bathroom. She closed the door behind her noisily and tried to slow her pounding heart. What had she just done? What Mark said in the car made so much sense, so why was she panicking at the finish line? Well, once she came out, she was certain he wouldn't be confused anymore about whether or not he was attracted to her. That would be the end of it, but she might still be able to salvage their work relationship.

Christina reached into her bag and pulled out the clothes she decided would represent what she normally wore. As Tina, she was wearing a black off-the-shoulder top and a brown corduroy skirt. She brought baby blue capris and a white fitted t-shirt. It was plain and ordinary and exactly her style.

She looked in the mirror. Her hair was horribly flat. Well, there was no reason why Christina couldn't be pretty after her own fashion. She started the water running in the tub and put her head under the stream. At least she could easily give her hair volume when it was short. She towel-dried her hair and then rooted around in Mark's medicine cabinet until she found his gel. Sure, she'd smell like him, but it was better than letting her hair dry without any product in it at all. When she was finished, it wasn't so bad. It was just herself and she didn't think she was ugly.

She clicked open the door and came out into the hall. Mark was in the kitchen. He was cutting up vegetables on a glass cutting board.

"Can I help?" she asked, coming into the room.

Mark turned and looked at her.

Christina wasn't sure how to read his expression. Was he disappointed in her and trying really hard to hide it? What was he thinking? "So, what do you think?" she got up the nerve to ask.

He smiled and then he started to laugh. "You know, this isn't what I expected at all."

"What do you mean? How could you not expect this?" Christina asked, indicating her appearance. "This is how I look every day at work."

"That's not what I mean. When I said that I wanted to see you change from 'Tina' to 'Christina' I was honestly expecting was for you to stand in front of your bedroom door, curtsy, go inside and come out again looking exactly like you normally do. But then when you said that you wanted to do it over at my place, I was really confused. From what you said, it almost seemed like you were going to try to seduce me, but what you had in mind was… different. I never expected you to practically throw your bra stuffing at me," he laughed.

"How is that funny?" she scowled.

"It's extremely funny. I don't have any sisters. I didn't see a crowd of teenage girls first thing in the morning after a slumber party. My mother is a very pretty lady who doesn't think it's her son's business to know anything about her morning routine. And to top it off, most of the girls I've been friends with would have died of embarrassment if I had seen them without their makeup. What you just showed me was… really eye-opening for me. I had no idea makeup did that much. Now I'm suspicious everyone looks completely different without it."

"So, you're not horrified?" she asked.

"No. I'm not horrified. I'm hopelessly intrigued that you manage to pull it off because you're right. You do seem to have a different attitude when you're 'Tina.' Come here and cut up the cabbage," he said, giving her a knife.

They shared the same cutting board. He cut up the onion while she cut up the cabbage.

"So, which one of us do you like better?" she asked nervously.

"Well, my apologies to Tina, but she's too cool to be real. You're perfect when you play her. Honestly, men drool over you from across the room. There's yet another reason for me to kiss you without breaking on New Year's Eve. Do you think I wanted every guy there trying to score a little time with you? No, ma'am."

"That's thoughtful of you," Christina said, blushing.

"I'm very thoughtful," he said, jabbing her playfully with his elbow. "But, I don't know if a person could really be as fabulous as Tina in real life. Something about it doesn't ring true; like a part of your personality is missing. You do an excellent job, but you turn yourself into a dream for a guy, like an actress or a poster girl. I guess that's why Dominic is trying to make you a model."

"Or something like that," Christina said clicking her tongue on her teeth. She noticed he left out what he thought of her—Christina—but she'd have to let that slide. It would be too humiliating to ask him about it twice. But she could ask him something else, "So, what was the deal with you and Laura anyway?"

"Nothing much. She chases me and I keep running. That doesn't mean I haven't got stuck going on dates with her once and awhile, because I have. It was just never as meaningful for me as it was for her."

"Why don't you like her?" Christina asked.

"I don't know. She's a nice person. She's smart, successful, well-connected, and sort of pretty, but I can't force myself."

"Why not? If she's all that?"

Mark thought for a moment before he answered, "Laura is very disciplined. She eats the way she is supposed to, works out as much as she is supposed to, votes, and visits her parents. I don't know how to describe it. She lives on a tight schedule. I can't live that way. If I were to get close to her she'd slide me into the appropriate time slots, and I'd just become another thing on her 'to do' list. I'd hate that. I don't want the woman in my life to hand me a number and ask me to wait in line."

"Makes sense," Christina agreed.

"The truth is I asked her to go to the New Year's party with me and she turned me down because she had an offer to go with someone else the January before. The guy who asked her completely forgot about it. He asked someone else in the meantime and he wasn't willing to break his date when he realized his mistake. I don't know why she believed him in the first place. Who's going to remember something like that eleven months later? So, after she found out her date had fallen through, she came and asked me to take her two days before the event. I was insulted she was using me as her last-minute life-line, so I lied and told her that I already had a date so she was on her own. Then I called your escort service."

Christina nodded. Yeah, that explained why Mark had called her agency. She smiled. It was cute that Mark's boss, Collin, had been the one to suggest it in the first place.

"Laura surprised me that night," Mark continued. "I didn't expect her to be so childish when I introduced the two of you. She must have been threatened. That made me think she liked me a lot more than she'd admitted, but I was still mad about being second fiddle to a loser."

"So, that's how she lost her chance to be with you?"

"I guess. I've tried to stay friends with her. She wouldn't be a good person to cross, but if she's really set on getting me then she's going to be disappointed," Mark said, scooting the vegetables off the cutting board and into the frying pan.

"What are we having?" Christina asked, looking over his shoulder.

"Oh! So fancy! I'm making you a stir fry."

"Yum!" Christina said enthusiastically.

Mark gave her a sideways glance. "You don't have to act so hyped up. Surely you've had men cook for you before."

"Actually, I haven't," Christina said as she checked on the rice. "Is there anything else I can help with?"

"Wash the bean sprouts, Princess," he instructed.

"Okay."

"You mean you've never had a guy cook for you before?" Mark asked.

"Nope," she said.

"I find that hard to believe."

"Well, when I'm working as an escort I'm seldom at anyone's home. I'm usually out with lots of people. None of my dates would dream of doing anything as nice as make supper for me. They're all worried that if they don't show up with a woman on their arm they'll look like losers in front of their friends. They're not actually trying to win me over," Christina explained.

"What about before the escort service? When you lived at home, one of your little boyfriends must have done something for you," Mark persisted.

"What boyfriends are you thinking of? You mean someone more significant than a nervous boy approaching me at my locker and asking timidly if he can be my boyfriend. If you mean something more than that; I haven't had one. No grand passionate love for me, and to be honest, I don't really see something like that in my future."

"Why not?"

"Oh, because I'm more like the girl-next-door than a hopelessly unattainable escort, so I don't think it will be possible. I'll probably date an average-looking guy who works in accounting for a respectable year, get married six months later, have three kids and die old and happy. Nothing special."

"Accounting? Do you already have someone picked out?" Mark suddenly flared. His back was to her as he flipped the contents of the frying pan.

"No," Christina denied. "I just mean I don't have any extraordinary plans for my life, but you're very sweet, Mark. You're the first man to cook for me."

"Put the spouts in." He sounded weary.

Christina did.

"So, where did you get the idea to go work for an escort service?"

"I already told you my cousin, Mindy, works for one. I was poor because I missed out on a scholarship and a grant. I ran out of money and if I didn't want to go home branded for life as a failure; I needed money fast. On my darkest day, Mindy asked me if I wanted to go to work with her and I said I would because it was my last chance to make enough money to pay everybody off."

"And did you?" Mark asked.

"Yep. I don't work for them anymore. I have my dream job working for the 'golden boy' of the office—"

"The 'golden boy!'" Mark exclaimed, interrupting her.

"Yep! All the girls ogle you. Didn't you know?"

"No."

"It's true," she said, taunting him. "I'm very lucky."

"And you really don't hope for anything more exciting in your life than being my assistant?" he asked, looking at her incredulously.

The look in his eyes confused Christina and so did his question. She didn't know how to answer, but she did know one thing without question. There was no way a guy like Mark would be interested in her if she was only 'Christina.' Her answer came out easily after she had that thought.

"Aw, Mark," she said. "I don't know what you're talking about. You don't think it would be exciting to bring a wholesome guy home to mommy and daddy? I promise you, it would be. Imagine if I took home a guy like Alexander or Dominic home. My parents wouldn't know what to do. If it were Dominic, they'd be afraid to talk because he'd think anything they said was stupid. You know, he's so obviously critical of everything; he'd sneer at them. If it was Alexander, they'd remember his commercials and advertisements and worry I'd sold my soul to Satan."

"How about me?" Mark asked boldly. "How do you think your parents would react if you brought me home?"

Christina almost squeaked. She hadn't thought about that. "Hmm," she said, trying to sound complacent. "I'm not sure, though I'm sure you'd do better than the Figura boys. What about me? How do you think your parents would react to me?"

"I think they'd—"

Just then the doorbell rang and interrupted him.

"Were you expecting anyone?" Christina asked.

"No," he said, turning down the heat under the vegetables and going to the door.

Christina followed behind him. She hoped it wasn't Dominic or something.

Mark looked through the peep-hole and looked at Christina. Then he sucked in his breath and opened the door.

"Hello Laura," he said when he saw the blonde.

Christina wanted to disappear when she saw the look of utter horror displayed on Laura's face. Why hadn't Mark warned her? She could have hidden in the closet.

"Mark," Laura said quietly. "I didn't realize you had company. I thought maybe we could have dinner." She was carrying takeout bags in her hands.

Mark frowned and said, "Well, if you don't mind having supper with the two of us, then why don't you join us?"

Christina's heart fell as he said it, even though she knew he didn't have much of a choice. If he sent her away, it might be considered the epitome of rudeness as far as their friendship was concerned. Besides, it wasn't like Christina and Mark were in the middle of a hot date.

"I don't want to interrupt," she said mildly, but still not budging from her place.

"You're not interrupting," Mark said smoothly.

"Well... if you're sure," Laura said as she stepped into the entryway and took off her shoes.

Christina followed the two of them back to the kitchen and bit her lip. Biting her lip as a reaction was mild. She wanted to roll her eyes back into her head in aggravation. She did not want to have dinner with Mark *and* Laura.

"Hey Christina," Mark said, trying to include her. "Would you mind setting the table?"

"I can do that," Christina said, feigning cheerfulness. She opened one of the kitchen cupboards to find the plates, but she opened the wrong cabinet and instead found rolls of paper towels.

"I'll do it," Laura said when she noticed Christina's blunder. "It'll be faster. I already know how the kitchen is laid out. Why don't you go sit down in the living room, Christina?"

Christina glanced at Mark before moving. She wanted to see if he was going to let Laura order her around like that.

He didn't say anything. He didn't even look at her.

"Okay then," Christina mumbled and went into the living room. When she got there, she saw her bra inserts lying on the floor and said a little thankful prayer in her heart that she got the chance to get them out of sight before Laura came in and saw them. With nothing else to do, Christina decided she might as well start gathering up her stuff. She had left her wig and other accessories on the living room couch. Charming! Mark's living room wasn't her bedroom.

Finally, Christina set her backpack by the door. It was an action Laura's watchful eyes didn't miss. Maybe she thought Christina had been planning to stay the night but had changed her mind because of Laura's appearance. Christina didn't care what she thought.

Christina was slowly getting an idea of the kind of person Laura truly was. She looked so regular and sensible that Christina had thought she and Laura must have a lot in common, things like common sense and regular female understanding. But the truth was that she and Laura had nothing in common. Christina would never have barged in on someone's date and demanded to be included. She also would never have asked her own brother to distract the girl her crush liked so that she could move in on the other girl's territory. The more she thought about what was going on, the more she felt her blood pumping irritably. What a sticky mess!

Christina sat down at the table and waited for Mark and Laura to finish up in the kitchen when she heard a ringing sound. It wasn't her ringtone, so she didn't even blink. It wasn't her responsibility to answer it.

It rang twice before Mark pointed out that Laura's pocket was ringing.

"Hello," she said cheerfully as she put the phone up to her ear. "Yes, she's here," Laura said, glancing over at Christina.

"Do you want to talk to her?" Laura covered the distance between them and handed the phone to Christina. "It's for you," she said.

Christina took the phone. Who could be calling her on Laura's cell phone?

"Hello?" Christina asked confusedly.

"Hey Babe," a mellow voice drawled plainly. "It's Dominic. How are things going? Having fun on your date with Mark?"

Christina turned around on her seat and pointed herself away from the kitchen. "Why are you calling me?" Christina asked nervously.

"Well, I thought maybe you might not want to hang out with Mark and Laura tonight. I wouldn't."

"So? What's it to you?"

"I'm waiting in my car outside Mark's apartment right now. If you feel like taking a job as Tina, I'll pay you five hundred dollars just to walk out of that apartment and get into my car," he drawled.

"What?"

"You don't even have to date me. I'll take you home if you want. Just let me offer you a little job that is clearly more profitable than staying there."

Christina bit her lip again. She never would have imagined that the devil would offer her an easy-out at such a convenient time. Yeah, she wanted to take him up on it. Five hundred dollars and a ride home? Did it get any sweeter? But what would she say to Mark? She'd think of something.

"Can you wait ten minutes?" she whispered.

"I'd wait hours," Dominic said suggestively.

"Great," Christina said and disconnected the phone. She turned around to see Mark and Laura standing on the other side of the table waiting eagerly to hear what her phone call had been about. Christina felt a sudden gush of dislike toward Laura and glared at her openly. "Mark, can I talk to you for a minute?"

Mark set the frying pan he was holding on a hot pad and nodded for Christina to follow him down the hall. "Sorry, hang on a minute," he said to Laura.

With that, he led Christina into a room beyond the bathroom and closed the door. Before the door clicked shut, Christina saw that it was a bedroom. It was Mark's bedroom. Was it okay for her to be here? She'd never been in a man's bedroom before.

The room was full of books and there was a desk with a laptop on it. His bedspread was light brown and the bed was sort of made. Maybe no one had ever taught him the proper way to make the bed, but the covers were smooth at the least.

He sat down on the edge of the bed and put his hands together. "What was that all about?" Mark asked, referring to the phone call.

Christina didn't answer his question at first, but instead started by asking, "Mark, are you aware of the awkward, awful situation you have put me in tonight?"

"What?"

"You said that you wanted to get to know me and I thought that this night was all about wiping the fairy dust off our eyes and honestly learning about one another. Now that you invited Laura, I have been completely knocked off balance. I left myself very vulnerable taking off my makeup in front of you and since you've placed me in this weird situation, I don't think you appreciate my sacrifice."

"What do you mean?"

"With Laura here, I don't know how to act. If you purchased me as an escort I would know exactly what to do. I'd just crawl all over you with my pretenses and phony flirting until she got frustrated and backed off, but since I'm here as myself, I am not confident or poised enough to compete with her for your attention. I thought part of the reason you brought me here was to give me the chance to be myself without the charade. Now that chance is spoiled."

Mark looked regretful and said quietly, "It's too late to send her away."

"Maybe," Christina said boldly. "But it's not too late for me to leave."

"What?" Mark scowled. "You wouldn't seriously leave before dinner, would you?"

"Of course I would. I don't have your feelings about social etiquette and unending politeness as far as the company is concerned. I'm not experienced in public relations yet. I have no problem walking out your front door and relaxing at home with a bubble bath and a glass of tonic water. In fact, I know I'd enjoy that more than watching Laura compete with me for your attention. Besides, Laura wants me to leave so she can have you to herself."

Apparently, Mark had no response to that. Christina thought he must know it to be true.

"Please don't go," he said at last.

"Do you know who called me just now?"

"I can guess it was either Alexander or Dominic."

"Dominic," Christina answered unflinchingly. "I don't think he would have called if Laura hadn't told him I was here."

"I don't think—"

"Don't be stupid," Christina interrupted. "Are you so dense that you can't see she is dead serious about getting you? Dominic has gallantly offered to remove me from this awkward mess and I'm going to let him."

Mark's eyes bugged open.

"I don't think he'll be so interested in me once he sees me without any of my frills and flounces. Do you?" Christina asked, crossing her arms across her chest.

Mark frowned. "I don't think it will make any difference to him."

"We'll see," Christina said, turning to leave the room.

"Wait!" Mark exclaimed getting up and grabbing Christina by the arm. "Is this the last chance I'll have with you?"

Christina didn't want it to be the end of their 'relationship' either, but at the same time, dinner with Laura? Not likely. "I'll give you my number. You can give me a call the next time you have some spare time."

"I already have your number," Mark said, still holding onto her arm.

"Then, I'm telling you it would be nice if we could do something together sometime. I'd like it if you called me. Regardless, I'll see you at work on Monday."

With that, Christina smiled and left the bedroom. She was pretty proud of herself. She'd done a good job telling him what she really thought.

"See you later, Laura," Christina called into the kitchen cheerfully as she went into the entryway and put her shoes on. "I can't stay for supper after all. Bye."

Christina had one last look at Mark before she closed the door. She wasn't sure, but she thought he looked frustrated. Well, he could be frustrated. That wasn't a bad way to leave things at all.

But as a direct result, she had to deal with Dominic. Oh! Goody!

Chapter Eight

Into His Car

Christina stepped onto the pavement outside Mark's apartment complex and looked around for Dominic's Jaguar. It wasn't hard to find because his car was the only one on the street with its headlights on. Christina went up to it and peered through the windshield at the driver. Yeah, with those shades, it couldn't be anyone else besides Dominic.

She reached for the car handle, but the door was locked. He had to be that kind of jerkwad, didn't he? She tapped on the window with her knuckles and Dominic unlocked the door. With that, she dropped her bag onto the backseat before getting into the passenger side herself.

"You really are the devil," Christina said nonchalantly as she hooked up her seatbelt.

Dominic took off his sunglasses and turned his body a whole ninety degrees to get a better look at Christina. "Tina, is that you?"

"Of course, it's me," she answered, flicking him an annoyed expression before turning her head resolutely toward the window. "Would any other woman get into your car and call you the devil without knowing you?"

"Hey, look at me," Dominic ordered.

Christina turned her head deliberately and looked him in the eye.

At first, she wasn't sure what his reaction to her regular appearance was. It was his first time seeing her as herself. There was no glimmer in his eyes or twist of his lips to indicate if he was pleased or repulsed. Mark said he didn't think Dominic would be put off by her real appearance, but Christina didn't know what Mark was basing that opinion on. It might be nothing. Was that why his car door had been locked? Because he didn't recognize her?

Finally, Dominic put his glasses back on and put his hands on the steering wheel. "You need a tattoo on your ankle," he finally said and Christina concluded he must think she wasn't 'all that' after all.

"Is that all you have to say? I was expecting you to be more critical," she sparked.

"About what?" he asked, turning the car onto the street.

Christina took a long-suffering breath before she answered, "About the real me. Shouldn't you be making some comment about how I'm not fit to be seen with you in public without my wig or something? If you hired an escort and you got me the way I look right now, you'd surely be disappointed. So, why not just say it?"

"You're right. If I called and asked for an escort to be my personal eye-candy and you showed up looking like that, I'd be disappointed, but not for the reason you think."

"Oh?"

"I'd be disappointed you didn't take your job more seriously. A certain amount of polish is necessary, don't you think? Right now, it sounds like you think I don't find you attractive because you're not covered in glamor. But, the thing is, you're making a mistake."

"I am?" Christina asked, astonished.

"Actually, I'm impressed you're so pretty without it. Not a lot of women are, you know, and I know a lot of female models who look like nothing at all without their mascara. I wasn't expecting you to be half as beautiful as you are now. I'm *very* impressed."

Christina was speechless.

"Besides, it was never your looks that interested me. I

told you before, I have never met a woman who was so good at reading my moods and giving me what I want. That's why I thought you were interesting and why I thought you might make a good model."

"Do you really want to become my agent?" Christina asked abruptly. It was the one question she wanted the answer to. Everything else he said was probably fluff.

"Not really," Dominic said, shrugging his shoulders. "I don't want to have that much responsibility regarding what you do. I'm merely offering this as an opportunity. If you want to make a big deal out of this campaign with Alexander, you might end up as a model instead of an office gopher, but that's up to you."

"So, why even suggest the 'opportunity?'" she asked, using his word. "Only because you thought I'd be good at it? That seems unlike you."

"It is. See what I mean about you reading me? You have a special talent. Are you sure you don't already know the real reason behind my actions?" he asked dangerously, turning a corner at high speeds.

"I don't know. Why don't you just tell me? We're alone."

Dominic abruptly maneuvered into a parking lot and stopped the car. Then he turned toward Christina and began hovering over her like a storm cloud. She felt like he was invading her space. "I can't believe how alike we are," he said darkly. His brown eyes shone over the rims of his red shades as he continued. "I'd like to tell you what I've got in mind, but... uh... I'm a little concerned you have your own motives through all this. If you do—I doubt they're the same as mine. Maybe we could both get what we want if we work together."

"I scratch your back, you scratch mine?" Christina asked smoothly, refusing to lose her composure or to be bullied by Dominic.

"Exactly," he answered calmly. "Hmm. I don't want to take you home. How about my place?"

"So we can talk about this in a more 'comfortable' setting?" Christina asked dryly.

Dominic touched his nose and put the car in reverse.

***

Christina wasn't sure if it was safe to go with Dominic to *his* place without a guardian or something. She didn't think he was the type to attack her, but he had acted so unpredictably in the past, she wasn't sure if she would put anything past him. In the end, she decided to go, because she wanted to hear what he had to say. She also had a nagging feeling in the back of her mind that said she still hadn't made it completely clear to Dominic that he didn't have a chance with her—either as a business partner or as a lover. She had to make him understand that before the end of the night and if he simply dropped her off at her apartment then it wouldn't get done.

Even after being in the luxury of Mark's apartment, Dominic's flat was more like a museum than a living space. There were thick woven rugs on the floor and actual statues placed on pedestals at regular intervals in the living room. Dominic lit the fireplace as soon as they entered, even though the weather outside was warm. Then he sat her down on a chair that was covered in animal skin. The walls were dark red and the paintings were clearly from the Renaissance. Christina felt like she had stumbled into the devil's private office.

"You haven't eaten yet, have you?" Dominic questioned warmly. "Would you like me to fix something for you?"

"You cook?" Christina asked incredulously.

"If cutting is considered a form of cooking," Dominic

said with a soft laugh.

Christina felt the skin on the back of her neck prickle at the way he said 'cutting.'

"Whatever is easy," Christina said stiffly. She had wanted to turn him down, but she found herself unable to. She was starving. It had been hours since her last meal.

Dominic asked Christina to wait in the 'den' as he called it, while he went to procure food. She offered to help him, but he said he wanted her to relax and absorb her surroundings, so she should stay put.

Christina did look around. There was an antelope head mounted on his wall. Even though she was from the country, she was still disgusted. She didn't think putting dead animals on the wall was tasteful even though she knew many men who hunted. She didn't think Dominic had killed the animal himself, but what if he had? Christina shuddered. Maybe it was better if she didn't know.

So Christina waited. The fire cracked and sparked and she thought about the room and what it said about the person who lived there. Christina didn't think Dominic was shallow. He appreciated wealth, but the culture of his apartment was simply beyond her experience. She didn't think Dominic intended to make her feel naive, but having her sit in his weird sitting room reminded her how inexperienced she was. She had probably bitten off more than she could chew following the devil home.

Dominic came back into the room in the middle of Christina's conversation with herself. He carried a tray, which he sat down on a coffee table. Christina thought about Mark's stir-fry and examined what Dominic had created. There was a glass dish with shrimp and cocktail sauce, three different kinds of cheeses on a plate, and a myriad of sliced fruit organized on a different plate. Yeah, he definitely knew how to cut.

"I've missed the last thing," he said blithely as he quickly returned to the kitchen. He came back with a bottle of tonic water and two Champagne flutes. "Did I get your tastes right?" he asked as he unscrewed the top of the tonic water.

Christina smiled and searched the tray for crackers. Noticing there weren't any and she found the nerve to complain. "Don't rich people eat crackers?" she asked, picking up a piece of cheese and putting it in her mouth.

"Of course," Dominic laughed. "How thoughtless of me. I'll be right back."

Apparently, he thought her demanding a cracker was adorable, and Christina wondered if she could do anything that would turn Dominic off. Well, once both of them spilled their guts, he would see how poorly the two of them matched up. Christina would have bet her falsies on it.

When he came back, they began eating together. Dominic sat on the floor with his back to an armchair. That way, the light from the fireplace illuminated one half of his face and the other half was left in shadow. Maybe it was intentional. He also undid the top two buttons on his shirt. Maybe his collar was choking him... maybe.

"I said I wanted to tell you my motivation behind making you a model. You must be able to guess one of the reasons," he said simply.

Christina couldn't forget he had interrupted her date with Mark no less than an hour ago so that Laura could spend some quality time with her object of desire. "Naturally, you haven't squared things off with Laura, so you're still doing her bidding."

"Yes."

"Care to explain why you owe her?"

"She wouldn't like that," he said before biting into a shrimp and ripping off the tail. "Besides, that has nothing to do with our current situation."

"Fine," Christina agreed, sounding like cool-headed 'Tina,' even though she was dressed like 'Christina.' "She likes Mark and for some reason she will be content with no other man. You are willing to help her because she's blackmailing you and so you casually offer me five hundred dollars to leave his apartment—which you still haven't paid me," she reminded him casually.

"I'll pay you when I drop you off," Dominic said. He even looked impressed that she hadn't forgotten about the money. "Yes, Laura is quite crazy about Mark. I can't see the reason myself, but—"

"She isn't going to get him," Christina interrupted.

"You're going to get in the way?" Dominic asked, looking intrigued.

"No," Christina said shortly. "She's still assuming I'm the barrier stopping her. In reality, it has nothing to do with me. He may have used me as a scapegoat to explain his waning interest, but it's nothing but a pretense. It won't matter how many of his girlfriends you dispose of. He's not interested in her."

"Well," Dominic said, raising his eyebrows. "What can we do to *make* him interested in her?"

"What? You can't seriously be asking me how to get him to fall for her."

"Why not? I think you have the skills to teach her how to to turn his head."

"Even if I do, it's not like she would take advice from me!" Christina rolled her eyes.

"I wasn't thinking you'd give her hints directly. You'd give them to me and I'd relay them to her—"

"Without telling her where they came from," she finished for him.

"Basically."

A brief silence passed before Christina said, "Look, it's

too late. He already has established ideas about Laura and her personality. Meaning, he knows her. More than a surface 'I met her at a party'. He knows her. He knows how her brain works, her habits, and he knows that her lack of charm is part of her character. There's no chance for a first impression or the thrill of meeting someone new. If she started using feminine wiles on him at this point, it would look gruesomely obvious. He would know something was up. He's just not interested. I think your time would be better spent trying to get her to land someone new."

Dominic cleared his throat and said stiffly, "You think I haven't tried that? It's Mark or it's no one."

"Well, what have you tried, besides repeatedly buying me? To be honest, I think you're backing into this from the wrong angle—probably because it's more fun for you."

"What makes you say that?"

"Well, just think. Has Laura ever been romanced? Has a man ever treated her the way I treated you on Valentine's Day? Has anyone ever gone out of their way to make her feel special and sexy?"

"I don't know," he answered slowly.

"If I were you, I'd hire a male escort for her, tell her it's a blind date, and give the escort specific instructions on how to treat her."

"That's no good. What if she falls in love with the escort?"

Christina sighed. "That's not the issue. The escort would merely be a transition man to get her heart off Mark. If she notices how the escort treats her compared to Mark (who doesn't do her any favors), then maybe she'll break out of her shell and start to think about other men. Ever think about that? And on the plus side, if charming Mark happens to see her with another man and experiences a twinge of jealousy then maybe your job will be over and she'll get him in the end anyway." Christina couldn't read the expression on Dominic's face, but the more she thought about it the more she thought it was a good idea. "I think it would work even better if you hired more than one escort for more than one date. Give her a whole string of men and instruct each of them to act slightly differently toward her. After a few dates, she'll believe there's a whole world of men out there she's never known about. With a bit of luck, she'll get a little daring and find herself a new man without wanting any more help from you."

"That's an interesting idea," Dominic said as he flicked his hair away from his eyes. "Except I don't really have the time to set all that up. Do you think you could help me?"

"Now I'm *your* personal assistant instead of Mark's? No thanks. I already have three jobs and apparently, I work weekends," Christina said, indicating she was working at that moment.

"Do you know?" he drawled. "I love every word that comes out of your mouth. That is a perfect solution to all this. If you became my personal assistant, I feel positive we could accomplish great things together."

"Please don't get excited," Christina murmured, putting her hand to her forehead. "I'm not going to stop working for Mark."

"Why not? I'll pay you—"

"I don't care about that," she interrupted. "I'm afraid that once I started working for you, you'd see how inexperienced I truly am. I might have come up with a few ideas you liked just now, but I'm not qualified to serve your every need. It might surprise you, but I don't know a lot about my profession yet. I'm an entry-level assistant. I only graduated from college in April. And," Christina said, grasping for ideas that would convince him of how unfit she was. "I don't even know what kind of cheese this is," she said, picking up a chunk. "So just forget about it."

"Hmm," he hummed. "Well, I see what you're saying, but I still think you would make me an incredible assistant."

"So, do you want to tell me the real reason why you set me up with this modeling job?" Christina asked, basically ignoring what he said. She had things she wanted to learn from him during their interview as well.

Dominic sighed. It was the most human gesture Christina had ever seen him perform. "Well, there were a couple of reasons. But I'm not confident I can explain them without hearing one thing from you."

"What's that?"

"Do you have a sincere interest in Mark? If he gave you the opportunity, would you go for him?" Dominic asked looking at her face carefully.

Christina's mouth hung open for an instant. She wasn't sure how to answer him, but having listened to Mark talk his way out far harder situations had paid off and a plausible answer came to her mind. "So far, he hasn't treated me very well. He should have sent Laura away when she showed up on his doorstep. The fact that he didn't when he was entertaining me was seriously offensive. I don't know if I want a guy who lets a girl he's not interested in walk all over him."

"Don't like playing second fiddle?"

"No."

"Neither do I," he said quietly. "I ask because it feels like you favor him over me, even though the two of us have this... unique connection."

Christina was touched by his voice and found a lump growing in her throat, but she still had to say what she felt. It was her way of spilling her guts. "You must know I can generate that connection with anyone. It's part of my job when I work as an escort. You have to be intelligent enough to know the name of that game."

"I know," he said, nodding his head. "I know, but somehow, the fact that it's fake makes it even better."

How could she answer that? A moment of silence followed before Christina cleared her throat and asked seriously, "Are you going to explain your other reasons for trying to make me a model?"

Dominic took a slow drink from his goblet before he answered steadily, "Certainly. You see, my dear brother Alexander is a very talented model, but representing him lately has been a rather unpleasant job. He's not an easy man to work with. You saw how cross he became back at Collin's office today. He's temperamental. In the past, his work has been so flawless that the hassle of having him pose has been worth it, but... his work hasn't been so perfect in the last year as to make him irreplaceable. Since his last photos came out, some of his clients are seriously looking at getting someone new. For me, it's okay if Alexander retires if he's tired of the business or even if he's got something else he wants to do. It's not okay for his popularity to dwindle and his work requests to disappear. I was thinking that if I got you to model with him for this campaign then maybe I could raise his stock and improve his reputation. You could tell a few reporters how much fun he was to work with, and I would be spared hours on the phone explaining to photographers that he's become more flexible. Right now, some of them refuse to work with him."

"What about Collin? Doesn't he mind?" Christina asked.

"Collin isn't afraid of Alexander's tantrums and he enjoys making him uncomfortable."

"This should be interesting," Christina groaned, thinking of how much fun it wasn't going to be to model with Alexander.

"Look, I wouldn't have recommended you for this if I

didn't think you could do it. It might surprise you, but I am a hell of a lot scarier than Alexander. I wouldn't have been able to push Alexander up as far as I have if I wasn't able to bully him. Trust me, if you can handle me, you can handle him."

"Okay," Christina said, expelling a heavy breath. "Is there anything else I should know?"

"I think I'm in love with you."

Chapter Nine

On the Couch

Christina pushed open the door to her apartment a little after midnight. She thought she was going to have to stay out with Dominic until dawn, but luckily, he believed her when she told him she was really tired after spending all week getting ready for her interview with Alexander. So, he took her home. He clearly knew how hard the week had been on her after a little explanation of Mindy's schedule, unlike Mark, who didn't know anything about women. When Christina thought about it on the car ride home, she wasn't sure if she preferred a guy who was so inexperienced with women that he couldn't guess how detailed her primping routine was or a guy who knew everything and therefore knew how to coddle her like a princess.

She also didn't know what to make of Dominic's 'almost' confession of love. She didn't know if he meant it or if he was just playing another game with her. She'd have to put the idea on the shelf and wait to see what his behavior was like in the future. There was something appealing about being treated like a goddess. She wondered if Dominic had the ability to make her feel like that—the way she'd made so many men feel working as an escort. No man had ever made her feel like that before. Well, at least he wasn't pushy. He hadn't grabbed her or forced her into anything, not even when he slid five crisp hundred dollar bills in her hand when they said 'good-bye.'

"Thanks," she had said to him as she opened the car door.

"Good night, Tina," he said. He was sans sunglasses and the look on his face was so tender.

Christina wanted to tell him that no one ever called her 'Tina' when she wasn't an escort, but then when she looked at him, she realized he wasn't calling her by her name. For him, it was the same as if he had called her 'darling' or 'sweetheart.' She didn't know what to say. In the end, she bit her lip, shut the car door as quietly as possible and went inside.

The TV was flickering when Christina entered her apartment. Mindy's work must have ended early if she was home watching television.

"I'm home," Christina called into the living room as she kicked off her shoes.

"Have a good night?" a deep male voice called from the living room couch.

Christina froze in her footprints. If she wasn't crazy, then Mark was waiting for her. Christina shook her head. She must be hearing voices. Mark wouldn't actually have come to her apartment, would he? Christina unfroze herself and popped her head around the corner. Sure enough, he was sitting on the couch. He had Mindy's afghan over his knees and he was holding the remote control.

"Mark!" Christina exclaimed. "What are you doing here?"

"You said I should call you next time I happened to have some spare time. Well, after Laura left, I had some spare time, so I called," he said easily.

"That still doesn't explain why you're watching late-night TV in my living room."

"You weren't home, but your cousin Mindy was. She's a charmer, isn't she? When I gave her my name, she said I could wait for you to get back."

"You mean… Mindy's not here?" Christina gaped.

"No, she's out."

Christina looked at Mark. Yes, she wanted to see him, but hadn't she suffered enough? That day had been the longest in Christina's history. She'd been under Mindy's care until her meeting with Alexander. Then she had her polly-wolly-crappy date with Mark and then her date/meeting with Dominic. She was fried. Even her eyebrow was twitching. Standing there, she had the impulse to throw Mark out, but as she looked at him she realized she couldn't do that. He had gone through so much trouble to show her he was sincere. Curse him...

So, instead, Christina plopped herself on the couch next to him and said drolly, "Did Mindy leave you with any good snacks?"

"She got me a bowl of... Hey! Is that all you have to say after I went through the effort to come here?" he shouted hotly.

Christina put her finger to her lips, "Please don't make so much noise. You'll wake the neighbors. Mindy will be mad at me if there are complaints."

"What! How can you be thinking about that?"

"Shhhh... Pass me those cheesies and let's find something good to watch."

"But weren't we supposed to be getting to know each other on a more honest level?" he asked, actually having the nerve to get up from the couch and bring her a can of pop from the fridge even though it was his first time visiting.

"Thanks," Christina said snuggling down with the root beer and not answering his question.

He stood, hovering above her, waiting for her answer.

"You read my mind. If I'm going to eat these, then I need a drink." She popped a cheesie into her mouth.

He didn't budge.

Finally, Christina felt like she had to give in. She rolled her eyes and said, "Look, Mark, it's after midnight. I'm exhausted. It has been such a hard day. Can't you just curl up on the couch with me, maybe put your arm around my shoulders if you feel like it, eat junk, laugh at stupid stuff, and relax? I can't have a serious conversation right now. I don't even think I'm capable of coherent thought right now. Can't you just mellow?"

"I can put my arm around you?" he asked cautiously.

"Why not?" Christina retorted. "You've already done more than that with me," Christina said, thinking of the New Year's party and their kiss.

He shook his head. "I know. It's just I thought maybe you wouldn't want me to touch you."

"If there's a reason for that, I can't think of it right now," Christina answered. Her mind was a complete blank.

"Aren't you mad at me because of what happened with Laura tonight?"

"Oh yeah," she said. Mark had invited Laura to have dinner with them without asking Christina if she was okay with it. Christina shook her head. "Yeah, you are pretty rotten. But... that's okay," she yawned. "We'll talk about it later."

Mark looked confused. "So for now, you just want me to sit on the couch, cuddle with you and watch T.V.?"

"I've got too much on my mind right now to let you add more. We can talk about everything later, but right now, I'm tired." She paused. After thinking for a second more, she added, "And I want to rest my head on your shoulder and don't you dare try to attach any strings to it."

Mark looked more confused than ever. "Are you drunk?"

"No, I'm not drunk," Christina fumed. She wasn't sure if he was trying to make a joke. "I don't drink—ever. I'm just past my exhaustion threshold. Did you know sleep deprivation is a form of torture? I'm done."

Mark didn't say anything else, but obediently sat down on the couch and put his arm around Christina's shoulders. She immediately put her legs over his lap and pulled the afghan over both of them. Christina was used to sleeping with the radio playing, so the noise from the TV didn't bother her as she rested her head half on the couch and half on Mark's arm.

Christina didn't start to have doubts about the intelligence of falling asleep in his arms until it was too late for her to struggle against it. She thought to herself that she should really get up and send him home or toddle off to her bedroom and leave him to sleep on the couch, but she was too tired to talk. Her last thought before she fell asleep was of the cologne he was wearing. What was it called again?

***

Christina woke up to the sound of the phone ringing next to her ear. Some thoughtless person had left it on the side table next to the couch rather than putting it back on the cradle. Christina fumbled around for it but knocked it onto the floor. It was Saturday and it felt too early for anyone to be calling them. Christina saw Mark's slender brown fingers effortlessly pick up the phone through her eyelashes. So, he hadn't gone home.

"Hello," he answered calmly.

Christina flinched. What gave him the right to answer their phone? Especially so early in the morning? What if it was her mother calling? But all the same, Christina was still nine-tenths asleep and she didn't much care. He could come up with something to cover his can if her mother jumped down his throat, couldn't he? Wasn't that what public relations were all about? Christina rolled over.

"No, Laura. I can't do anything today," he paused.

When she heard Mark say that, Christina flipped to only one-tenths asleep and listened carefully. It was at that point she woke up enough to realize the phone that rang wasn't her home phone, but Mark's cell phone.

"No, it doesn't bother me," he continued. "You can date whoever you like." There was another pause as Laura answered him. "If Dominic found a guy who he thinks would interest you, then you should go on the date and see how it turns out. You might end up liking him."

Christina sat bolt upright and looked at Mark. What was he saying? That Dominic was setting Laura up with someone? Wow! The devil didn't waste any time.

Mark had his back to Christina as he continued his conversation. It looked like he still thought Christina was asleep because his voice was almost a whisper. "I'm sorry you don't want to date anyone other than me, but Laura, how many times do we have to have this conversation? I'm tired of offering excuses. Please, just give up on me." He paused again. "No, this doesn't have anything to do with Christina. I just—" He was interrupted.

The moments stretched before he had the chance to talk again. Christina waited tensely for his next words.

"Please don't cry," he said gently. "No, I don't think there is anything you could do to change my mind. I said I don't want to talk about this anymore. Just please believe me when I say I'll never change my mind, but I'll always be grateful for our friendship."

Christina had never been dumped as harshly as Mark was dumping Laura. At first, she felt proud of him for finally saying what he had been thinking all along, but it didn't take long for that feeling to evaporate. It was obvious it wasn't his first try breaking up with Laura. It probably wasn't the second time either... and Laura was crying on the other end of the phone. Self-assured Laura from Financial Services was shedding tears because Mark didn't love her the way she wanted him to. Christina couldn't imagine liking someone that much.

"I'm sorry," Mark said, clearly finishing up the conversation. "Please stop crying and let's try to talk normally when we see each other at the office, okay? Let's not let that part be awkward." There was another pause before he finally said mildly, "Goodbye."

Mark clicked his cell phone off and turned around to meet Christina's gaze. "Did you hear all of that?" he slowly questioned.

"Yeah," she mumbled.

"Did it bother you?"

"A little, but don't worry about me. You've already said I'm not the reason you're rejecting her, so I don't feel responsible. It's just a shame her feelings had to be hurt. That's all."

He squinted and brought his eyebrows together in a line. "Christina, I don't understand you. Wasn't the reason you took off your makeup in front of me because you didn't want your escort glamor tainting my feelings for you? Because you wanted me to fall in love with the real you? If you want to date me yourself, then why do you feel sorry for Laura?"

"You wouldn't fall in love with me, Mark. The real me isn't flirty, or frilly, or vivacious. The real me is more like what you saw last night. I'm not the type to manipulate a guy into treating me the way I want him to. That's just an act Mindy taught me so I could work as an escort. You probably want a woman who pouts her lips, has to have her way, wears pretty clothes and bothers to dress up for you every day of her life. What I really want is just to be able to say what I want, what I don't want and for my man to give it to me. I never thought you would fall in love with me. You are stacked up to your chin in class and you want a woman who can match you. I never could."

"So, are you interested in me or not? Sounds like not," he said pensively.

"No. That's not it," Christina denied fiercely. "You have got to be the hottest man I have ever seen in real life. Everything about you makes it seem like you were designed to break my heart. Just by looking at you—I know it's a dream. There's no way you could care for me the way I truly am. I'm the type who drools over you in my cubicle while you are the type to date a woman with real eyelashes, flowing hair, and a body that would make grown men cry. Do you know what I'm saying?"

Mark plopped himself down in Mindy's recliner and looked bored. "It sounds like you're spouting the most elaborate load of B.S. I've ever heard."

Christina scowled. How could that possibly be the most elaborate load of B.S. he'd ever heard? He made up crap worse than that daily.

"What happened after you left with Dominic last night? It must have been something terrific for you to change your tune so drastically."

"I'm not 'changing my tune,'" Christina almost shrieked. "Besides, I didn't act differently after I met with him and found you in my living room, now did I?"

"Well, you didn't want to have our 'serious' conversation and… you fell asleep on my arm," he reminded her. "That wasn't my idea. I'm almost starting to feel like your whore, or at the least, I feel like I was a tool you used for convenience."

Christina's mouth fell open. She had never been accused of using a man for her own purposes. "I didn't…"

But Mark interrupted her. "Listen," he said stiffly. "There is one way to test out the waters of your little theory about the 'type' of person I am since you clearly don't know me well enough."

Christina was ultimately perplexed. What the heck was he about to suggest?

"And that's if you agree to be my girlfriend. Then we'll see how much of what you just said is fact or fiction."

Christina flushed, but managed to say nicely, "How will it go at work if we start seeing each other?"

Mark shrugged his shoulders. "Nothing will change."

"Are you sure?" she demanded sternly. "You were pretty freaked out before when you were worried there would be a scandal."

"Yeah, I was, but I see now that was pretty immature of me. Trust me; there won't be any trouble with Collin."

"How can you be so sure?"

Mark sighed. "Because he already thinks we're dating."

Christina's mouth fell open and stayed open. What had Mark done? It didn't fit in with the picture she had drawn up of him. She didn't know what to say, but at last, she found her voice enough to ask, "And how did he get that idea?"

Mark shrugged. "He just assumed after we met in his office, when I told him you were the escort I hired."

"And you didn't correct him?" Christina blurted.

"Why would I correct him when I want to date you?" he said evenly, meeting her eyes with his steady gaze.

Christina's heart fluttered. She was speechless.

Mark lifted himself out of the recliner and came over to the couch. He got down on his knees in front of her and put one arm on either side of her. Their eyes met.

She squirmed. He didn't understand. He had no clue how she felt even though she tried to explain it. She was trying to protect herself from getting hurt in the worst possible way, and he was on his bleeding knees. He couldn't see the disaster in store for her heart if she dated him. She would see him every day, work with him every day and in her young, naive way, she would begin to think of him as hers. She'd see the slight bend in the muscle of his arm and think, 'That's my boyfriend.' Or she would hear someone in the office talk about him and think, 'They're talking about my boyfriend.' Or he'd bend to kiss her and she'd fall head over teakettle for him and believe there was a future before them. She would believe all these things so completely she wouldn't even recognize it when the relationship was over. When he dumped her, it would be devastating. She'd probably die of the shock. And he would walk over to some other girl sitting on the couch and say he wanted to try out a relationship with her instead. He'd be fine, but Christina would never recover. She would stay dead and never, ever feel alive again.

"Christina," he said quietly. "Sorry, I accused you of using me. I don't feel used. It was cute of you to fall asleep on me. I want you to do it again… tonight… tomorrow night—anytime you want. Just pull down your carefully constructed layers of reserve for me—just for a little while—we'll learn all about each other and I'll show you how well we fit together."

His voice was so persuasive that even though Christina was certain it was going to turn out to be a fatal mistake, she couldn't open her mouth and tell him to leave. Finally, she nodded her head and let him take her out for breakfast.

Chapter Ten

The Perfect Man

Christina sat across from Mark in a tiny booth in a downtown diner. She had never been taken out for breakfast before, so being there with him was a totally new experience for her. She ordered pancakes and drummed her fingers impatiently on the surface of the table while Mark looked over the complimentary newspaper.

He looked up at her quizzically. "You seem nervous. What's the matter?"

"You're an idiot," she blurted.

"Really?" he asked, hardly able to keep his mirth in check. "You know, Christina, you have this way of lashing out at me for no explicable reason. It's intriguing. So tell me, why am I an idiot?"

"I already explained that dating you would be like a dream come true for me. I know you don't believe me, but it feels one hundred percent impossible for us to be sitting all chummy like this at a restaurant. I'm having a hard time believing it."

He stared at her but said nothing.

"Sorry if I feel like I've been dropped on my head, but I'm still recovering from the shock."

"You're a weird girl. Can't you just be happy that something so stupendous has happened to you?" he asked sarcastically like he didn't believe for one second that it was honestly a dream come true for her for the two of them to be a couple. "From my perspective, I practically had to hunt you and even still, you might split at any moment. I was thinking before we left your apartment that I might have to tie you up to get you to give me a chance."

Christina rolled her eyes. "Yeah, you're still thinking I'm Tina, the escort, and it's impossible for you to get me. I keep telling you—that's not me. If you asked me to marry you today, I'd take you up on it… if I wasn't absolutely certain that you harbor some extremely false, funny ideas about me. You're going to feel awfully stupid when you realize you have to dump me because I'm not what you thought I was. But don't you worry; I won't even say, 'I told you so.'"

"Okay," he drawled disbelievingly as he picked up the paper again and opened the business section. He scanned through the headlines quickly and then folded up the paper and put it behind the menu stand. Christina had already spent enough time with him professionally to know there was no way he could miss checking out the business section no matter what was happening in front of his face. "I think you're wrong," he said finally. "But let's not talk about this anymore. I still have a lot I want to learn about you and if you keep yowling we're not right for each other, I'll never learn anything."

"What do you want to know?"

Mark clicked his tongue on his front teeth and leaned forward with his elbows on the table. "What happened with Dominic last night?"

Christina frowned. She should have known he would ask something like that instead of something about her. How could she answer him? It seemed like a bad idea to tell Mark that Dominic offered her five hundred dollars to ditch him the night before, and she had taken it. Likewise, it seemed stupid to tell him Dominic had asked her to take a job as his personal assistant and he'd told her that he loved her. Ouch! She'd forgotten all about it until that very second. Christina's frown deepened. And then there was Laura's involvement. Christina still believed Dominic wouldn't have gone so far for her if Laura hadn't asked him to. Since he owed Laura he had to do what she said. Christina tapped her toes under the table and prepared to answer Mark's question.

"I'm not a tattletale. Besides, it doesn't have anything to do with you or me," she said.

"I don't think I understand what you mean. If Dominic took you out than it has everything to do with both of us."

Christina sighed. Mark had been there through those two dates with her and Dominic, so he thought he knew what the two of them were like together. He didn't know how they talked when they were alone and how different it was. The conversation would be easiest if Christina could just talk about Laura's problem and say what Dominic had told her instead of worrying about the love issue. But she didn't know what Mark already knew. She'd have to probe him. "How much do you know about Dominic and Laura?" she asked cautiously.

"They're twins. Alexander is their older brother, but I was under the impression that they were only born about thirteen months apart, so in many ways, they are all the same age. I've known Laura for about a year and a half," he paused. "I'm not sure what else to say. I already told you I find her hopelessly programmed. As for Dominic, I have only met him on half a dozen occasions, but he strikes me as an incredibly tough character. He'd have to be to put up with Alexander."

Christina nodded and began to say slowly, "Do you think that it was a coincidence that Dominic asked for me to be his date on Valentine's Day?"

"Huh?" Mark gaped.

"Laura asked him to hire me so you wouldn't be able to. Did you know that?"

Mark looked like there was suddenly something sour in his mouth. "I *should* have known."

Suddenly Christina's heart took courage and continued. "That was what Dominic wanted to talk to me about last night. He wanted to ask me about the best strategies to either get you to fall in love with Laura or to get her to change her mind about you."

"What did you tell him?"

"I told him there was no way any amount of time or inducement would win you over. I advised him to hire a male escort for her. From your conversation with her this morning, it sounds like Dominic has already taken my suggestion and arranged a date for her."

Mark gaped. "You can't be serious."

"I am. Professionally, I thought that would be the best solution. Not because I want you myself, but because you don't bend-over-backward for Laura. I thought if she was taken out by a heartthrob who treated her like a goddess then she'd realize the distinction between your feelings for her and concentrated consideration."

Mark's face became clouded and Christina was positive she'd offended him.

"Please try not to take that the wrong way," she said quickly. "It's just that you're not interested in her and she may be confusing your mild friendship for something more. She needs to see how a man acts when he's infatuated, not friendly. I mean, have you ever volunteered to make supper for her?"

"No."

"That's the sort of thing I'm talking about. Not that you're a jerk or that you don't know how to treat a woman properly. I think you do. It's just that it's clear by the way you stared off into space at the restaurant on Valentine's Day that you weren't thinking about her."

"I was thinking about you."

A blush rose on Christina's cheeks like a soaring hot air balloon.

"Oh, come on," Mark said, examining her expression. "You can't tell me that no one has ever said something like that to you before. You're supposed to be an experienced dater."

Christina put a hand to her cheek and glared at him. "Yeah, I keep telling you that's not the truth about me. And for your information, usually a guy who takes an escort out isn't thinking about how to treat her nice, he's thinking about how she can treat him nice. That's why I thought Laura would do better with a male escort as a rebound date rather than an ordinary guy. Ordinary guys are stupid."

"Do you know a lot of male escorts?" Mark suddenly asked as their food arrived.

"No. They don't hang around the shop much. I think it embarrasses them. The girls like hanging out and talking, whereas the guys like to be on the other side of the world."

"Huh… I wonder what type of guy Dominic will choose for Laura."

"It would be fun to see him choose the perfect man for her, eh?"

***

Christina thought Mark intended to spend the whole day with her, but he got an urgent phone call from his brother and had to take off after breakfast. Christina knew she shouldn't feel happy he was going, but being with him was a little intense and the break would relieve mountains of tension. When he said goodbye to her, he kissed her on the forehead unassumingly and told her he wanted to take her out for dinner that night, so she shouldn't schedule anything. His business with his brother wouldn't take all day.

When she came into the apartment, Mindy was on the phone laughing her head off. "Christina, get in here," she yelled.

"What is it?"

Mindy took the phone away from her ear and said merrily, "You just keep getting into trouble, don't you?"

"What are you talking about?" Christina questioned.

"Has your little pet boy gone home for the day?" Mindy asked, biting the phone's antenna.

"Little pet boy," Christina quoted, her eyes wide. She couldn't believe Mindy had the nerve to refer to startlingly hot Mark that way, but apparently…

"Yeah, is he gone?"

"Yes," Christina answered sternly.

"Well, then maybe you can help a certain gentleman down at the escort service. Apparently, he's trying to pick a male escort for his sister and he can't sort through the files at all. He says he needs your help or he'll never get anywhere. Feel like helping him out?"

Christina's eyes bugged out. How could she possibly weasel out? It was her suggestion. "Hmm… is he paying me?"

"I'll drive you," Mindy said sportingly even though she was clearly making fun of Christina. She smiled like a Cheshire cat and dangled her car keys in her left hand.

Christina put a hand to her forehead. She was completely stuck.

***

This shouldn't take too long, Christina told herself as she and Mindy drove down to the agency. *I can just help him with the lineup of guys and then I can go home and get ready for my date with Mark.*

Once inside, Christina saw Dominic standing at the counter flipping through a laminated catalog with all the agency's listed escorts. Naturally, the female side of it was much larger than the male, so he was only turning about twenty pages over and over again.

When Christina came in, he turned around and said, "Great, Tina, you're here. I can't look at this."

"Why? They're not naked or anything," Christina offered unhelpfully as Mindy smirked and trotted off to the back.

"Who's that?" Dominic asked, glancing at Mindy. He was not rattled by Christina's hectoring.

"That's my cousin, Mindy. She's an escort here. Didn't you see her profile?" Christina asked, taking the catalog from him and flipping to Mindy's page.

"No. I didn't look at the girls."

"But aren't you going on a double date with Laura tonight? Have you already asked a girl to go with you?"

Dominic was slick as a cat's ear as he responded, "I was going to ask you."

"I'm not in the book anymore," Christina answered calmly.

"Does that mean you're unavailable?"

"Yes. But, I will help you pick out a group of escorts for Laura. It sounds like a lot of fun."

"But you won't come with us?"

"No."

"It would make Laura feel better about everything if she knew you weren't with Mark."

"But," Christina said before taking a deep breath and continuing. "I will be with Mark, and maybe you should tell her that. The information might help her figure out that Mark isn't available anymore."

Dominic's face became dark. He understood the significance of that statement as he bit, "He sure gets up early in the morning, doesn't he?"

Christina knew she had slipped up. She should have just let Dominic find out about her and Mark through the office grapevine when the news got to Laura. Instead, she had been honest and Dominic clearly felt gypped.

"I'm sorry," Christina started to say.

Dominic shrugged his shoulders. "Don't worry about it. Like you said before, Mark's not so great. You'll see it once we start working on the ad campaign together. He won't have any idea how to treat you once that ball is rolling. For tonight, I'll take out your cousin, Mindy, if she's available. She's going to be doing your hair and make up for the ads, isn't she?"

"Maybe."

"Great. I can at least talk shop to her and the evening won't be boring, but I still want you to help me pick out a date for Laura."

Christina took the catalog and sat down on one of the waiting chairs with Dominic beside her. Together, they flipped through the pages. At first, Christina didn't think she had a better idea of who to pick than Dominic would have if he had been left to do it alone.

"Well, we should eliminate all the ones younger than twenty-four," Christina said thoughtfully.

"Okay, but that doesn't leave a whole lot."

"No, it doesn't," Christina said, "but we should also eliminate all the guys older than thirty-four. If he's too much older it'll look strange." Then she opened the rings on the binder and pulled out the remaining sheets.

"That doesn't leave much," Dominic said, looking at the profiles.

"Yeah, there are only six left. Let's see. There's Gregory, Daniel, Vaughn, Michael, Shane, and Gavin."

"They sound like a boy band," Dominic commented crossly, looking away.

"Don't be so depressing. This guy, Vaughn, is sort of cute. Clear blue eyes, ponytail, and the sheet says he likes adventures. I think he'd probably have a hay day with pretty, polished, perfect Laura. Opposites attract, right?"

"I think she'd tell him to get a haircut."

"Okay, then someone more made up. Hmm… what about Gavin?"

Dominic glanced at the picture. "He's a pretty boy and not only that, but he looks exactly like Laura. I'm in the modeling business and I've never seen a guy with hair like that. Besides, she'd never go for a guy who is her carbon copy with a stick shift."

"Right," Christina said, stuffing the sheet back into the binder. "Then I think that Gregory and Michael are your prime choices, but I happen to know that Michael is pretty popular and it'll be hard to get him. We'll probably have to schedule him in advance if you want to line him up for a date in the future."

"I want to see how tonight works out before I set up a schedule. I guess we'll go with Gregory," Dominic said wearily.

Christina got up and talked with the receptionist, but quickly returned to the chair beside Dominic. "It looks like Gregory is booked for tonight, and it goes without saying that Michael is. His schedule is booked solid for the next two weeks."

"Every night for two weeks? What is the man—"

Christina interrupted him before he finished that thought, "Look, I saw him once. He clearly knows what he's doing, but he's probably not the best bet for the first night out of the gate. He's too intense and too perfect at what he does. I think you should book him now, even if tonight doesn't work and get him to take Laura out later on."

"Fine," Dominic said aggressively, like he was already tired of the escapade. "But who are we going to get for tonight if both those guys are taken?"

"There's Daniel and Shane, but if Laura doesn't like long hair than Daniel is out. However, I don't think Shane is such a bad choice. He's blond with big honest eyes. He looks like the boy-next-door, so he's probably had plenty of women cry on him before. I'll bet he knows all about healing a broken heart."

"But is he available?"

The receptionist, obviously listening to their conversation, smiled and said, "Yes, he is. Would you like me to put a request through to him?"

"Right away," Dominic said impatiently.

"We need to talk to him though," Christina interjected as the receptionist started dialing. "He'll be dating a girl with really specific needs and so he has to be careful in the way he treats her."

"How does he need to treat her?" Dominic asked curiously.

Christina thought for a second before she responded, "He needs to know that she's upset about Mark and feeling bad. He needs to pay attention to her body language and look carefully into her eyes when she talks about what's wrong like he really wants to hear. Then when he gets a chance to say what he thinks of everything Mark did, he should be noisy about how he would *never* treat a woman that way and give a length, descriptive explanation about how he *would* treat someone he cared for. And he should bolster her confidence by complimenting her and letting her know how desirable she is."

"Wow..." Dominic mouthed.

"Then after Shane," Christina continued, "if it works out to your satisfaction, you should get Gregory, but his instructions should be different. He shouldn't be comforting her. If she's constantly being consoled than she won't be able to stop thinking about Mark, so her date with Gregory should be all about distraction. You should know the kinds of things that interest her and would get her mind off Mark."

"What about her date with Michael? What should that date be like?"

"Well, I don't think you should double date that night. I think she should go on her own. Michael is smart. By the end of the night he'll probably have her purring. He should wake her up to the idea she could be happy and attracted to someone who isn't Mark."

"So, what do I do when those three dates are over?"

"Set her up on a date with a guy who isn't an escort and see how it goes."

"And what if she falls in love with one of the escorts and is furious when she can't have him?"

Christina sighed. "That's a risk," she stated baldly.

"Okay," the receptionist said. "Shane's booked."

Dominic got up and made the final arrangements. He also booked Mindy, so everything was settled. When they were finished, Dominic said he had to go. He still had some things to do before the date that night.

"Wait," Christina said, calling him back with only her voice. He was such a decisive guy she wasn't sure if he'd stop, but he did. He carefully turned and looked at her through his yellow tinted glasses. He stood there waiting patiently for what she had to say. "I just wanted to know if you meant what you said earlier."

"About?"

"The photo shoot," Christina stammered.

"What about it?"

"It sounded like you thought Mark wouldn't be able to handle watching me model, or manage me."

"I meant it. There's no way you'll still want him by the end of it. I promise. See ya later, Tina," he said coolly as he disappeared onto the street.

Chapter Eleven

A Photographer is Worth a Thousand Words

Christina couldn't get what Dominic said to her at the escort service out of her head. He said, 'There's no way you'll still want him by the end of it. I promise.' Where did that kind of arrogance come from? But that wasn't the only problem. It wasn't just Dominic's attitude that bothered her. It was the fact she knew what he said was true. She and Mark couldn't last, so when Dominic said those words it felt like he saw straight through her. Naturally, it was an unpleasant sensation.

It wasn't that she wasn't interested in Mark. She was. It was just that she couldn't shake the idea that he liked her false face better than herself. If he just enjoyed having her around because she could put on a good show, then everything she was afraid of would happen when he got bored of her. She'd be brokenhearted and, on top of any other fallout, she'd feel like a fool for having trusted him.

Without question, Dominic understood her alter ego wasn't real, and for some weird reason, that made all the difference in the world to her.

It had only been a few hours since she had agreed to date Mark, but already she felt like she had made a mistake.

Not that Dominic was any better. He was clearly the devil, but he made her see that she could get someone who wanted her exactly the way she was. She didn't have to settle for someone who was impressed with false eyelashes.

It wasn't until later that afternoon that she got a phone call from Mark. He explained that he wasn't going to be able to shake off his brother for supper and asked her if he could tag along with them. Christina scratched the back of her neck and said she didn't mind. She didn't tell him the remainder of her thoughts, that she thought him inviting his brother was an extension of his bad behavior with Laura the previous evening. Couldn't he explain to one person he had other plans and they would have to wait?

Needless to say, she didn't put a whole lot of creativity into her attire that night. She wore a pair of blue jeans, layered a low black V-necked shirt with a white tank top, and put on her black boots. She decided her makeup didn't matter, so she only wore eyeliner, mascara and lip gloss.

When the time came, Christina went onto the balcony and watched for Mark's car. She was half daydreaming when she spotted something interesting. There was a car pulling into her building's parking lot, but it wasn't Mark's Toyota. Instead, it was a Champagne colored Mercedes convertible and Mark was sitting in the passenger's seat. Christina's eyebrows went up. The person in the driver's side was apparently his older brother, but... what was he driving? Then Christina remembered Mark said his condo was actually owned by his older brother and his comments about rich relatives.

Mark got out and started walking toward her building.

But Christina thought it was stupid for him to ring her bell when she could see him, so she leaned over the balcony railing and yelled, "Hey Mark!"

Mark craned his head back and looked at her. "Oh hi," he called at half the volume with which she had called him.

"I'll be right down," she yelled even louder. Then she turned around and ran back into the apartment. She grabbed her keys and wallet and chased out the door. Some kinds of youthful exuberance just couldn't be hidden.

Outside the building, Mark was leaning casually against the side of the Mercedes with his arms across his chest.

"Hi," Christina said as she hugged Mark briefly.

"Christina, I'd like you to meet my brother, Trevor," Mark said, easily slipping his arm around her waist and turning her to face the driver of the car.

Christina smiled politely and said, "Nice to meet you."

Trevor took off his sunglasses and extended a hand to Christina before he said curtly, "Well, get in, girl, and make sure to sit in the front seat. I'm not escorting the two of you around like I'm your driver."

Mark opened the door for Christina and saw her seated before he hopped into the backseat. Christina couldn't help but wonder if Dominic would have gotten into the back for her. She doubted he'd even let another person drive.

As Trevor drove to the restaurant, Christina got a better chance to look at him, but it was hard to examine him properly without feeling like she was checking him out. Why didn't the man dress properly? He was wearing a white button-up-the-front shirt, which wasn't skanky on its own unless you happened to forget to do up the top five buttons and Trevor had forgotten. He wore several silver chains around his wrist and dog tags around his neck. Christina thought he was almost as handsome as Mark, except that his hair was cut so badly. Did anyone still wear their hair long in the back anymore?

When Trevor noticed her looking at him, he quickly asked her, "Is the wind bothering you?"

"No," Christina said, turning away and feeling embarrassed.

"No, I guess it wouldn't. I have a scarf in the glove compartment for women, who don't want their hair wrecked, but since you've got a haircut like that, then I guess you don't need it. It's a relief really. I can't stand the complaining."

Christina didn't even realize an open car would destroy a girl's hairdo, but once she thought about it, she conceded to herself if she had worn her wig, they would probably have ended up searching for it on the side of the road.

"You're not a womanizer, are you?" Christina asked him, suddenly flirtatious. Escort habits die hard.

In the back, Mark started laughing.

"Shut up," Trevor shouted at Mark with a chuckle in his throat. "For Pete's sake, can't a guy…"

Mark shoved his head between their seats. "Open the glove compartment, and we'll see if he's a womanizer or not."

"Don't do that," Trevor advised, trying feebly to stop Christina from getting it open.

But since he couldn't do much while he was driving, Christina easily clicked it open. It was crammed full of scarves. She pulled them out to get a better look at them. There were floral designs, stripes, and transparent ones of every color imaginable. She saw one that was such a pretty color of emerald green. She stretched it out to have a better look at it only to realize that it wasn't a scarf, but an incredibly brief nightgown.

Trevor was watching her out of the corner of his eye, and he started shaking his head ruefully as he saw what she discovered. "I forgot that was in there."

Christina started cramming the scarves back where they belonged when one of them was torn from her hands and blown out of the top of the car onto the road behind them. "Oops!" she cried.

"No need to worry," Trevor said unconcernedly. "I think that one was pantyhose."

"It was NOT!" Christina hollered over the wind and trying desperately to see what had happened to it.

"Look, we're here," Trevor said as he turned the car into the parking lot of the restaurant.

"I don't think that was very funny," Christina said getting out of the car. "Whatever happened with that woman, you should at least give her nightgown back."

Trevor shook his head thoughtfully, "If only I could remember which girl it belonged to."

"What!" Christina exclaimed.

"Trevor's not really a womanizer," Mark interjected as he pushed her seat forward so he could get out of the backseat. "He's just teasing you. He's a photographer. It might interest you to know he's the one who'll be doing your campaign with Alexander. The nightgown was probably leftover from a shoot and got stuffed there because there was nowhere else to put it."

Christina stood with her hands on her hips. She wasn't sure she believed him about the nightgown. If Trevor was really such a chaste guy, she bet he'd have a few more buttons on his shirt done up.

"You're the model who was chosen to pair with Alexander?" Trevor suddenly asked incredulously—like he didn't know.

"Yes," Christina answered, taking Mark's offered hand and going into the restaurant. "Is there something wrong with that?"

"No," Trevor said, before he took charge and arranged for a table for them with the hostess. When they sat down in their booth he finished his thought by saying, "No, there isn't anything wrong with that. It's just that I had a conversation with Dominic about the woman he was hoping they'd get before the decision was made."

"Trevor has a meeting with Collin about the campaign on Monday," Mark explained as he picked up Christina's menu and cuddled up to her. "What would you like?" he asked. He was clearly trying to draw the conversation away from the topic at hand.

Christina looked at him with her lips parted. She wanted to press Trevor and find out what Dominic said about her, but Mark wouldn't like it one bit if she *had* to know what the devil had to say.

"What are you ordering?" she asked, almost choking on the words as she said them. Then she took the menu very firmly in her hands and investigated it like it was the most interesting thing in the world.

It was lucky for her Trevor wouldn't let the subject drop. "Wait a second. 'Tina' is short for Christina, right?"

Christina nodded and said, "I think I was the only person Dominic recommended."

"I was expecting someone different," Trevor admitted.

Mark was annoyed. He clearly didn't want to talk or think about it and he put his arm on the booth above Christina rather than holding her. "Fine," he said like he had resigned himself to his fate. "What did Domi say?"

"Nothing much, but his description kind of indicated someone extremely exotic with a personality strong enough to squelch Alexander's."

"Is that even possible?" Mark asked.

Trevor shrugged his shoulders.

"Is Alexander really that hard to work with?" Christina asked, remembering what Dominic had told her back at his apartment.

At first, neither of them looked like they wanted to answer her.

"Come on," she persisted. "It's not like you're telling a journalist who's going to write an article. I'm going to be working with him. It can't be such a bad thing to give me a heads up."

"Regardless, I don't feel comfortable commenting," Trevor said stiffly. "It wouldn't be professional, but Mark here can say whatever he wants."

"Only as her agent," Mark finished, turning to look at Christina. "Alexander has a history of being difficult. He's spoiled. I've never seen it firsthand, but his fits of ego and drama have made headlines."

Christina frowned, "Dominic already explained all that to me. I was sort of hoping that you could give me an example of bad behavior."

"You'll just have to wait and see," Trevor said. "No doubt it'll be a surprise, but don't worry. Mark and I will be there to protect you—Dominic too. I'm sure he doesn't want a blood bath any more than the rest of us."

Christina looked at the menu, but she couldn't focus on it. Dominic thought she would make a good model because she would be able to sense what the photographer wanted and if Trevor was the photographer then she would have to please him. Suddenly, she thought to start asking him questions.

"What sort of concept do you envision for the ad campaign?" she asked, looking across the table at Trevor.

Trevor appeared amused as he answered, "Well, I haven't got all my thoughts together yet. My meeting with Collin isn't until Monday and I have to work with what he has in mind."

Christina nodded thoughtfully and said, "Sorry, you probably don't want to talk about it on a Friday night when you're not supposed to be working, but I have never posed as a model before and I'm really worried that I won't be able to deliver quality shots."

Trevor smiled and examined his menu, "Yeah, I heard you worked as an escort. That's a very interesting profession, but if you can convince Dominic you can do it then you probably can. He knows a lot about this business."

"Do you look down on me, because that's how I decided to put myself through school?" she asked abruptly because it seemed like he might be laughing at her.

Trevor cleared his throat and answered steadily, "Well, I've done a lot of campaigns where it felt like the product being sold was sex. I can't say I'm comfortable with that kind of business, but at least I know my models are only on paper and no one believes for one second they can actually be with one of them. The business of escorting someone seems different. It seems to me that business takes something like the image I create and takes it to a different level; to a real person a customer can see and touch. That's the part that makes me uncomfortable. Hopefully, no one actually believes they can be with their escort. It's a game, but after the experience is over, the customer has a memory of a real woman who held his hand and danced with him. He can remember her fragrance and the feel of her breath on his cheek. It would be hard for a lonely man to put the memory aside and he may never get someone equal to the escort in a real relationship. The damage might be irreparable. To put it bluntly, it seems like a dangerous game to me."

"How would you know how a lonely man feels? You probably have all sorts of desirable women fighting for your attention daily," Christina countered.

Trevor inclined his head like he agreed, but then he said, "Yeah, a model can act like she's made of gold when she's in front of a camera lens, just like you can act like you enjoy the company of the man you're escorting, but the truth behind the facade is seldom as pleasant as the act. Needless to say, I don't care for models. My last two girlfriends were personal assistants without the faintest hope of becoming models themselves. And even though neither of those relationships worked out, at least I never wonder whether they really cared for me. They were honest women without the slightest hint of pretension."

"Then you do look down on me," Christina finished, fighting to get control of her emotions. It would be terrible if she cried.

"Not at all," Trevor said, reaching across the table and grasping Christina's fingers in a way that suggested he was used to touching women and consoling them. "Mark told me about the trick you pulled over at the apartment when you took off your wig and were determined that he should know you for who you truly are. As long as you can keep sight of that, then you haven't compromised what's real for the synthetic." Then he let go of her hand and said smoothly, "I think I'll have the prime rib. Have you decided what you want, Mark?"

With those words, that particular conversation was over.

***

When Mark dropped Christina off at her apartment he stopped in front of her door and said, "Now you see why I couldn't leave Trevor at home tonight. He was one hundred percent determined to meet you."

"Even though you didn't tell him I was the model who got the job? He wanted to see what kind of girl I was because I'm your new girlfriend?" Christina questioned, positive Trevor's speech had only been to ensure Mark wasn't going to get jerked around by a bratty girl. It made her less angry at him and more sensible to his good points, even if she found his immodesty embarrassing.

"Something like that," Mark said, scratching the bridge of his nose. "Sometimes he's not a very reasonable guy. I wanted to be alone with you tonight. I'm sorry that our date was messed up by bringing him. I wish there was something I could do to make it up to you."

"It's okay. We see each other all the time. I'm your assistant, remember? As long as Lewis boys have a thing for personal assistants—I'm in. Right?"

"But I feel like everyone is conspiring to keep us apart."

At that exact moment, Trevor honked his car horn to hurry Mark.

"See what I mean?" Mark complained. His eyes looked tired. "Can I see you tomorrow?" he asked, taking hold of her hands.

Christina didn't want to appear like she was thinking about it, but she was. She was exhausted from the weekend's activities. Finally, she answered, "As long as you don't have anything grandiose planned. I'm really tired and I need to mellow or I'm not going to be any good to you at work on Monday."

Mark smiled and said gently, "How about a date in a hammock with a cold drink and a book."

"Are you going to supply all that?" Christina asked.

He put his arms around her, "Just so long as you realize you won't be in that hammock alone. You can even nap if you want to. I'll let you use my arm as a pillow," he offered tantalizingly.

Christina felt the blood rushing to her cheeks. He was trying so hard to be nice to her. It was irresistible. "If that's what you have in mind, then you can pick me up whenever you want."

"Good," he said, as he bent down to kiss her.

Chapter Twelve

Model without a Cause

"Okay, everybody!" Collin boomed at the front of the darkened boardroom. "As you all know, we are going to be advertising Capier's brand new line of cell phone products called Clickmark."

A picture of a mauve colored cell phone appeared on the screen along with a list of features.

"This is the concept I have in mind for the campaign. The setting will be an urban metropolis. We will follow a basic storyline, with four or five still pictures comprising the plot. If the layouts look good enough to impress the big wigs, we'll start production on a commercial before the still photos are released. Hopefully, we'll be all ready to go by the beginning of November—just in time for Christmas."

Christina shifted in her seat. For some reason, she wasn't feeling very comfortable. Maybe it was the fact she was jammed between Dominic and Mark at the furthest arch of the oval-shaped table. She could hardly see Collin's face and she was having the worst time listening to him. Mark was fidgeting, shifting his weight, and glancing over at Dominic and Alexander every ten seconds. Whereas Dominic was sitting perfectly still. One of his hands was sprawled across the side of his face like a spider. He was biting on his pinkie finger. Apparently, he wasn't having as much trouble concentrating as Christina and Mark, but even so, Christina had an odd feeling he wasn't thinking about Collin's presentation. He had probably sat through a million such meetings. Instead, Christina felt like he was only thinking about her.

When Dominic caught her looking at him, he purposefully turned his head and winked at her. He resumed his thoughtful pose when Christina looked away.

The arched table in the dark was quite full. Alexander and Trevor were sitting together on the other side of Dominic, and Mindy was there, too. Then there was a costume designer, another makeup artist for Alexander, two of Trevor's assistants (one of which was an extremely smart looking girl in her mid-twenties), Collin's assistant, and one or two other people Christina couldn't account for. It was a full house and she was the star of the show.

At least, she felt like the star of the show. She had to dress up as Tina for their only full meeting before shooting. It almost felt like a dress rehearsal even though she had no lines and the only thing she had to do was show up. It seemed like everyone else had something important only they could do. She felt like she was a blank piece of paper and she needed someone else to write on her before she would be of any value. And yet, she was the star and receiving far more attention than Alexander, who was a pro in the business. Christina wasn't sure, but she thought he looked resentful.

Up at the front, Collin continued, "Tina and Alexander will be in the role of lovers playing hide and seek in the city with our new line of products. We hope to make it playful and sexy with an emphasis on the feelings of excitement a young woman could feel when the guy she likes gives her a call on her cell phone. These are cute phones and we want the female market from teens to grandmas. It's Alexander's job to look like the unattainable guy who suddenly can't wait longer than twenty seconds to call Tina. He's *that* attracted to her. It's Tina's job to look like the girl who's bursting out of her skin at the mere idea of our darling Alexander calling before three days have eclipsed."

"So, this is like the... opposite of reality?" Christina blurted, unable to control herself. She doubted Alexander would call her after three months, let alone the standard three days.

A flurry of laughter erupted along both sides of the table.

It was too late by the time everyone laughed for Christina to realize she had made a deadly mistake. She made it sound like she would be the last person in the world to get butterflies in her stomach over Alexander. "I just meant he would never call me," she grumbled.

"What are you talking about, Tina?" Alexander said, reaching past Dominic to take her hand in his. "I'd call you the day after."

Dominic flicked Alexander's hand away and muttered crankily, "She's taken."

Collin put a hand to his mouth and pretended to cough before he said in a crystal clear professional tone, "Tina, if a guy is really interested, he really will call right away. You have to look like the kind of girl that would make a guy want to call without waiting. Do you think you can do that?"

Christina shrunk down in her chair. Yeah, she had definitely put her foot in her mouth. She guessed it wasn't very mature for her to be cracking jokes when she had never done any modeling before. They were taking a chance on her, so she needed to have a better attitude.

She wanted to apologize, but taking back what she said seemed a little childish, so instead, she straightened and said calmly, "I'm counting on you to help me be exactly what you want. I'll try my best."

Collin smiled as if to say he accepted her non-apology and then he went on to list the locations for the shoot. One would be on the city streets outside a coffee shop, another one would be in an underground train station, and the last one was in their own office.

Alexander groaned when he heard the last one. "You're not going to make me pose in your office again, are you? Haven't we been through this already?"

Collin nodded. "Yeah, we've been through this before. If you're not interested in doing those shots, then Tina can do them by herself since she's being so cooperative. Photo editing is amazing these days. Wouldn't you agree?"

Alexander turned away grouchily and refused to answer.

"Well, you can think about that," Collin said crossly. He closed the laptop that displayed his notes and asked his assistant to turn on the lights. "Now we'll talk about logistics. Trevor will be presenting this segment." Collin took a seat and Trevor stood up to take over.

Trevor didn't get far into his portion when Christina lost her ability to pay attention. She didn't understand a word he was saying. Apparently, the upcoming portion was more for the benefit of everyone besides Christina and Alexander, the two who only had to show up and look pretty.

Maybe Trevor was right and modeling was different than being an escort. She had to appeal to everyone who might look at the photograph instead of just one man. She stole a glance at Mark, the one man she *had* to appeal to. He seemed very interested in his brother's portion of the presentation, since he had completely given up fidgeting. It didn't feel like he was thinking about her the way Dominic was, because she was positive the devil's mind hadn't wavered.

***

After the meeting, Mark and Christina got separated. He was talking with Collin and Trevor while Christina's only route was to leave the building with Mindy. Christina wasn't expected to work as Mark's assistant on days when she was working as Tina, so she only had to make an appearance at work during the morning for the meeting. It was noon and she and Mindy were planning on eating lunch together in a restaurant down the street. At least, that was the plan until Dominic commandeered them.

He was on the street outside Capier's building putting Alexander in the back of a limo when he saw Christina and Mindy step out of the building. Abruptly, he shut the door on Alexander and banged on the roof of the limo to let the driver know it was okay to go without him. Then he turned on his heel and approached Christina and Mindy.

"Good work today," he said to them both cheerfully. By that point, Mindy and Dominic knew each other rather well. He took Mindy with him on both his phony dates for Laura's benefit. At least they knew each other well enough to be friendly.

"You too," Mindy said, echoing his sentiments.

Christina gave him a dirty look. What was he doing here? "Aren't you supposed to be with Alexander?" she asked grouchily. "Won't he be mad at you for blowing him off?"

"Dang! Was I supposed to escort him out?" Dominic smiled as he watched the limo disappear around a corner. He shrugged his shoulders. "Too late now. I'll catch up with him after I take the two of you to lunch."

"We already had plans," Christina said, trying to make her casual lunch with Mindy sound like something important. "You can't just cut in on them at the last minute."

Mindy rolled her eyes and made her feelings known before Dominic had a chance to argue. "Didn't you hear what the man said, Christina? He said he was going to *pay* for both of us to have lunch with him. Did I not teach you anything? Not to mention if we go out with him, we'll probably get to eat at a restaurant where we don't have to carry our food to the table ourselves. Catch my drift? Let's go, Dom." With that, Mindy put her arm through Dominic's and let him lead them down the busy street.

Christina was left to trot meekly behind them—scowling. She couldn't help it. She didn't like Mindy's way of talking openly about being a sell-out in front of Dominic. Christina guessed Mindy didn't care because it wasn't like Dominic didn't know what she was. Why bother with the pretense of being someone you weren't? Christina wished she could be that honest—except not in front of Dominic. She had the feeling there was more to lunch than he said. She couldn't forget what he said to her weeks ago at the escort service. He hadn't given up on her.

Once at the restaurant, Christina got to hear a detailed account of Laura's dates with the male escorts. Christina had heard a little from Mindy before, but it was more interesting when Mindy told the story with Dominic because then she got to hear both their perspectives at the same time.

"Shane was tough, even though he looks like a sissy," Mindy said brazenly when recalling Laura's first date.

"Tough?" Christina asked. She couldn't imagine sweet, blond-haired, blue-eyed Shane being anything different than a little brother type. "How could he be tough?"

Dominic shook his head, "Well, you said he should get her to confide in him and to tell him about her troubles with Mark. Naturally, she didn't want to. He was patient though and chipped away at her defenses until she finally pulled him aside to talk to him. I guess she told him everything because when we found them, she was crying her eyes out on his shoulder and he was…"

"Patting her head," Mindy finished, unable to wait for him to do the honors.

"Really?" Christina asked, not quite able to visualize the scene even though it had been her idea in the first place.

"Yeah," Dominic said, looking as surprised as Christina felt. "I still can't get over how well it worked out, but I guess she was a little extra sensitive because she knew you were out with Mark."

Dominic looked into Christina's face to see her reaction to that observation, but Christina refused to be rattled. She maintained that it didn't matter if she existed or not, Mark would never have fallen for Laura. So, she waited for Dominic to go on and eventually, he did.

"She even asked to be set up with him again since they missed exchanging cell phone numbers. After that, we took her out with Gregory."

"How did that go?"

"I think Laura was disappointed it wasn't Shane again," Mindy said, gulping her water.

"Yeah, it felt like we were pitting Gregory against both Mark and Shane which would have been cruel."

"How did he manage?"

"We went to an amusement park because it was supposed to be 'all about distraction.' Remember?"

At that point, Mindy started to laugh. "Gregory is a riot. I didn't know him too well before, but man alive, I want to find out all about him now. You'll never guess his superpower!"

"Superpower?" Christina repeated, stunned.

Mindy took a deep breath before she answered carefully, "It seems that in a past life, Gregory was a carny."

"A carny?" Christina exclaimed.

"That's right," Mindy giggled. "He used to be one of those guys who stands there at the carnival and shoots paper targets with a BB gun. You know, the person running the stand who can actually score enough points to get a really big prize. That way, everyone thinks it's easy. So, Gregory found the game he used to run and he won Laura this gigantic pink spotted frog within the first ten minutes."

"No way!"

Mindy shrugged her shoulders, "Then he took her on the roller coaster and kept her moving until it was time to go. They even got their picture taken together in a booth. I was surprised that Laura had enough stamina to keep up with him, but then his energy is infectious. That must be why he's so popular."

"Wow," Christina said, completely dumbfounded. "Her next date was supposed to be with Michael, right? Has she gone on that one yet?"

"She went on Saturday… by herself," Dominic said meaningfully.

Christina leaned closer to him across the table and whispered, "Did she tell you how it went?"

Mindy leaned in to listen as well. "Yeah, tell us."

Dominic looked at both of them twice before he spun his sunglasses between his fingers and answered, "I'm not sure she'd want me to tell you."

"Come on!" Mindy groaned. "Haven't we been your partners in all this? Christina cooked this all up and I went with you on those two dates. Come on! Spill!"

"I don't know," Dominic continued, sighing and appearing to be torn.

"You can at least tell us if it went well or not, right?" Christina encouraged. "If it's super personal, then yeah, don't tell us the details, but you can at least let us know which way the wind blew. Right?"

"Well, it didn't go as well as you expected it to, darling Tina. Michael was a little smoother than Laura likes. Yeah, from her description, it sounded like he knew what he was doing. His moves sounded smoother than butter. To be honest, I sort of wanted to go beat the crap out of him after what Laura told me. But he was supposed to be the last escort-made date, so I think it is okay to let it slide."

As Dominic talked, Christina remembered the next phase of the plan. They were supposed to set Laura up with a real guy.

"Do you have any plans for who should be her next date?" Christina asked seriously.

Dominic frowned for an instant before he flourished a fantastic smile and said, "That's why I wanted to ask you two out for lunch. We need to talk about something."

"Ask," Mindy said acting like whatever Dominic was going to say involved her as much as it involved Christina.

"I have someone in mind for her real date, but it involves putting you, Tina, in a rather awkward situation when you're already going to be stressed. Mindy, you have to help her."

Christina's body suddenly felt hot and uncomfortable. From his tone, she knew it was going to be something she wouldn't like.

"Explain quickly, Dom," Mindy said in her sternest voice which was anything but inviting.

"I want to set her up with Trevor. I think they'd match. It's just that Laura will need to be on-site during the shoot from time to time. You know, to make sure that the two of them see each other a little before I suggest they go on a date. Do you think you'll be able to deal with her daggers, Tina?"

Christina stared at him with utter revulsion. He really was the devil; horns and everything.

***

Christina's first instinct was to ask Dominic if he was punishing her for choosing Mark over him or if he was truly a sadist at heart. If Laura hung out on the set it was going to be a thousand times worse than just an 'awkward situation.' First of all, her presence was completely unnecessary, because she worked in financial services and not in marketing. Second, Christina didn't think it was professional for Dominic to invite family members on a shoot. After thinking up those two reasons, Christina's brain short-circuited and a score of other reasons flooded and clogged the logical part of her consciousness. Mark would be uncomfortable. Trevor would be working, and if Laura hung all over him, who knew what the consequences might be—not just for him, but for the project?

In the end, Christina's eye twitched. Then she got up and said smoothly while looking down at Dominic, "You're asking for too much. It seems like you're trying to wrap up all your problems in a week. You have to have a man for Laura. You have to make Alexander more popular before he ruins himself. You have to torture Mark. You have to torture me. It's too much! If only you could buy that much with a simple lunch." She paused and looked into his eyes. "Well, you know what, Dominic?"

"What?" he said softly like the wind had been knocked out of him.

"I've just thought of a new mandate for your growing list."

"Go on," he said when she paused.

"Convince me you're not the devil, because I'm through helping you. If you want to bring Laura on the shoot, knock yourself out. If she glares at me, she glares at me…" Christina paused and inhaled. "You know what I think you're really doing? I think it's not Trevor you have your eye on as a prospective boyfriend for Laura. It's Mark. Neither one of you has gotten him out of your scope, even after our plan has been carried out and you want me to tolerate it. Otherwise, why tell me? You want me to stand there, pose with your brother, and tolerate her hitting on Mark in front of me. And I'm supposed to be so spellbound by this golden modeling opportunity that I don't notice the scheminess of my boyfriend getting stolen from me when it's right under my nose. The stupid part is that you think you'll still have a chance with me after I get dumped. That's the *real* plan, right?"

Dominic didn't say anything, but his expression denied nothing.

"And you expect me to think you're better than Mark? Ridiculous!" Christina grabbed her handbag. "Do what you want Dominic, but I'm through with you."

Christina swiftly marched through the restaurant doors with her cheeks on fire. Was 'scheminess' even a word? Whatever! She was right about him. He was the personification of hell, but if Mindy was so desperate for a free lunch she could stay. Christina didn't hear her cousin jumping up and running after her.

***

Christina didn't know what Dominic's reaction to her downpour had been. His face had shown no sign, so she was surprised when it came in the form of a summons to Collin's office the next day—without Mark.

Christina felt unusually nervous as she took the elevator to the Marketing floor and was waved in by the receptionist.

"Come in and close the door," Collin said when she knocked at his office.

Christina obeyed and sat down on the zebra-patterned sofa. "Is something wrong?" she asked timidly.

He looked at her curiously. "Can I ask you a question?"

"Anything," she told her boss's boss.

"Do you want to be a model?"

The question took Christina off guard. At first, she didn't know what to say. It was a full minute before she made the connection that Dominic must have done something to encourage Collin to speak to her. "I never had any particular aspirations to become one," she finally answered.

"Why did you agree to do our photoshoot then?"

"I thought it would be fun."

"But you didn't have any plans to try to make it as a model?"

"No."

"The reason I'm asking," Collin said, putting his feet on his desk. "Is that you have seemed really dedicated to doing a good job, and yet I just got a phone call from Dominic. Apparently, he has changed his mind about whether or not you're capable of standing up with Alexander and he is willing to provide me a detailed list of female models he thinks more qualified than you."

"Yeah, he would say that," she said bitterly.

"Dominic doesn't usually make professional recommendations as personal favors, but I suspected in your case he may have made an exception. Though at the time, I did not question why. Physically, you are good enough to stand up with Alexander, no matter what back-peddling Dominic is doing now. Can you give me a reason why Domi has changed his mind about you?"

"He found out I wasn't exactly what he supposed."

"I don't understand. You make it sound like you two were scheming something together. Care to come clean?"

"We were scheming something, but not what you think. I never told him I wanted to be a model or anything like that. He bought me a couple of times when I worked for the escort service, but he was only impressed with my way of reading his moods. He told me that was the reason why he thought I would make a good model. I was willing to go along with it because it's an interesting opportunity and at first it seemed like he didn't want anything in return."

"What does he want?"

"He wants his sister Laura to get together with Mark, or else he wants to see her happy with someone else—like Trevor. He spoke to me about it yesterday at lunch. Apparently, he 'owes' her or something. And he both wants me in the way and out of the way, but—I can't bet my life on what he really after. He's killing me."

Collin looked thoughtful for a moment and then he said, "Dominic kills everybody. The main concern here is whether or not you're willing to put your whole heart into our campaign. I don't care if you want to make a career out of modeling, but I do care that this one thing goes right. It's not too late to get someone else if you don't want to do it."

"No, I made a commitment and I'll try my hardest," Christina said, trying to make herself sound more convincing than she felt.

"And you'll be happy when it's time to go back to being Mark's assistant?"

"Of course!"

"Of course," Collin echoed slowly. "For a second there I forgot the two of you were in a relationship. But if Dominic and Laura are involved, the drama must be oozing. Don't tell me anything more about that. I'll get Mark to give me the details later. Right now, you should go back to him." Then his face cleared and he took his feet off the desk and walked Christina to the door. "Don't worry about Dominic. I'll deal with his complaint. He can't flip-flop on his recommendations. We don't *have* to hire Alexander."

Christina left Collin's office feeling relieved and uncomfortable at the same time. Why had she said all that stuff? Surely Collin wasn't interested.

Later, as she updated a database on her computer screen, she realized exactly why she was so ticked off with Dominic and why she had made such a good choice choosing Mark. She would never be able to trust Dominic. Even when it seemed like he was doing her a favor, he would always be manipulating things to his own ends. He didn't love her if he could only prove his love by lying to her and scheming.

She peeked around her monitor and saw Mark talking on the phone in his office—smoother than silk. Yeah, he could still sweet talk the pants off any corporate executive.

At that moment, Christina started to question where all her efforts were getting her. Could she really trust Mark more than Dominic not to cheat her?

Chapter Thirteen

Shooting the Breeze

The photoshoot had been scheduled for midsummer and the weather outside was beastly, but because the ads needed to look like they had been taken in the fall or winter, Christina and Alexander's wardrobe selections were extreme. Alexander was stuck wearing a dark gray sweater and a Matrix-style ankle-length overcoat while Christina was wearing thigh-high black suede boots. Trevor kept on talking about texture, so she was wearing a tweed skirt, an exceptionally shiny cream blouse, as well as an overcoat that wasn't completely unlike Alexander's. Trevor had seen the shots of Christina wearing the scarf and decided they needed one as a prop as well. It was boiling hot out. Christina couldn't see how she was going to make it through without making gigantic sweat stains through her top, though she didn't dare say anything to anyone.

She sat in a makeup trailer with Mindy fluttering behind her and a gigantic mirror in front of her. Alexander was two feet away snoozing in his chair. His hairdresser was using a straightening iron to make his long hair as smooth as silk. As if it wasn't already! The trailer had air conditioning, but it was only a matter of time before they were out in that blazing sun. Christina didn't know how Alexander could be so relaxed.

Christina hadn't seen Mark for a total of fifteen minutes that day. She saw him in the office that morning before she had to get going. She was disappointed.

Their romance had been... Christina didn't know how to describe it. She wasn't sure if it was going well or not. To be truthful, she hadn't ever been in a serious relationship and so she didn't know if the feelings she was experiencing were signs of real love or not. Mark was kind to her, attentive when she had his attention (granted, getting it wasn't always easy), and she felt goosebumps when he touched her and when they kissed. Yet, even with all that, she didn't feel comfortable. Yes, she had fallen asleep on him that night at her apartment, but after closer evaluation, she felt like it had been an act of sheer exhaustion rather than a sign she was more comfortable with him than anyone else. She hadn't been able to fall asleep on their hammock date. She hadn't been even a little bit drowsy. She sensed Mark had been disappointed she hadn't been more comfortable. He seemed to want them to accelerate the pace of their relationship, but too respectful of Christina's feelings to monopolize her time. It was clear he thought she wanted space.

The first location for the photoshoot was outside the coffee shop. Christina was supposed to lean against a brick wall, hold a cell phone and smile warmly while Alexander was supposed to be inside the coffee shop looking at her through the window. Christina thought it sounded simple enough. She was also delighted to see Trevor had set up a few fans, not only to give her hair a slightly wind-blown effect but also to stop her from fainting from heat exhaustion.

Alexander gave Christina a reassuring smile as he stepped into the coffee shop to take his position by the window. Christina was surprised. She thought he was supposed to be difficult to work with. He seemed easy enough to her.

Mark, Collin, and Mindy came to wish Christina well before they took up positions behind Trevor and his crew.

"Break a leg, or an arm, or a camera lens," Mindy said sheepishly before she hustled away. It was clear she was a little overwhelmed by the glamor of working on a real photoshoot. From Christina's conversation with Mindy the night before, she knew sugarplums were dancing in her head. Her cousin couldn't stop thinking about where the job might lead if she did it well.

Collin didn't say anything much. It wasn't that he didn't want to be encouraging, but Christina knew he had his hands full. He was a busy man, putting out fires. Laura showed up on the set just as Dominic warned and Collin had gone to talk to her before she got anywhere near either of the Lewis brothers.

Mark came up and said quietly. "You know, I have been thinking about what you said about being two-faced."

Christina smoothed the straying strands of her wig and nodded. "You mean the act I put on when I'm working as an escort?"

"Yeah. You keep saying it has nothing to do with who you are as a person, but I think you're wrong," he said, and as he spoke his eyes seemed somehow darker and more intense.

"Oh?" Her eyebrows slightly rose in interest.

"I think your ability to morph into whatever is needed in a given situation *is* part of you. It might not be the part closest to your heart or the part I need to win over, but it's the part of you that's going to carry you through your entire life," he paused. "And, incidentally, help you get through today, which, by the way, is going to be unpleasant at best. Alexander is a handful. Work hard and if it gets too rough, let me know and I'll intervene. You don't have to talk to me. Just give me a look, at least I'll get you a break."

Christina gulped. Was Mark beginning to understand a part of her she didn't understand herself? She had never considered the idea that everything she did—whether real or pretend—contributed to the person she was growing up to be. She pushed the thought out of her mind and focused on the professional part of what Mark was saying.

"I don't think Alexander will be that difficult. He seems to want to work with me. He just smiled at me."

Mark shrugged his shoulders. "Yeah, I don't know that him smiling at you means anything. Today is a day of surprises. Did you see Laura? I wonder what she's doing here."

Christina was tempted to tell him Dominic's plan but bit her tongue. After all, Collin was dealing with it. Besides, Christina thought smugly, he wasn't going to get any of the things he wanted. It didn't matter what Laura did. Mark wasn't for her. Plus, Christina didn't think Trevor was the type to try to romance Laura in the way the schooled boys from the escort service had. He just wasn't that type of guy. He was more of the take-it-or-leave-it variety.

"I'll try my best," Christina said, speaking again of the photoshoot.

"That's my girl," Mark said encouragingly. "After this, I want to take you for dinner if you don't have any plans."

"Do I have to come like this?" Christina said, indicating her appearance.

Mark smiled mischievously. "Only if you want to."

***

If Mark had a crystal ball that let him see the future, his prediction of how the day was going to go couldn't have been more accurate. Everything happened exactly the way he said it would. It started out easy. Alexander was in the coffee shop and she was standing outside, so because they weren't near each other, Christina couldn't do anything to offend him. However, once they moved onto the next series of poses, she couldn't do anything right according to Alexander. She did what Trevor told her to do, but apparently, her 'interpretations' of Trevor's instructions were all wrong. It went something like the following:

Trevor would say something like, "Alexander, put your forearm against the wall and lean into Tina. Take your right hand and take a strand of Tina's hair between your fingers, but don't let go of the cell phone. Got it? Now Christina, let Alexander pin you against the wall and look at him like he's your entire world. Hold your cell phone to your heart with your left hand and... bite your lip."

Christina would put her hand to her heart (cell phone in tow), bite her lip and try to look at Alexander like she was a blushing girl with all kinds of hopes tied to Alexander. She would even begin to feel her cheeks get warm when suddenly—

Alexander would pounce on her. He would look directly into her eyes and then he would say something like, "Trevor, I'm just not getting the feeling like I'm her *entire* world."

"Shut up and look pretty," Trevor would say caustically and the flash from his camera would start going off like mad.

Alexander would break pose and move away from Christina while exclaiming something along the lines of, "This just isn't working. I'm not getting the vibe from her that Collin described in the meeting. She's not working with me."

Then Christina's cheeks would flush for real and she would find herself saying something like, "Come on, Alexander, and let me try again." But it didn't really matter what she said or how hard she tried, Alexander just kept right on saying she wasn't doing it right and she wasn't easy to work with.

At around ten thirty he stormed off to the trailer almost screaming, "She's just NOT model material."

At a moment like that, Christina half expected herself to burst into tears, but she couldn't help but feel like Alexander's temper tantrum had nothing to do with her. He was just a freaking brat! Either that, or Dominic told him he had to make things as difficult as possible in order to discredit her. Yeah, she could see Dominic doing something like that. It was just like him. But, that would mean a partial loss of Alexander's reputation. Was Dominic really willing to sacrifice something that important just to spurn her?

And where was the devil in that critical moment?

Christina spotted him approaching the trailer. He didn't quite make it to the steps before Trevor got to him and reproached him. Christina couldn't hear their conversation, but it was clear that Dominic was getting told off. Christina had never seen Dominic cowed by anyone and apparently 'scary' Trevor didn't intimidate him either. He never lost his composure. In a cool attempt at collaboration, they ended up going to talk to Alexander together.

After the door closed, Mark came up to Christina and slipped his fingers around hers as subtly as possible. Christina doubted anyone noticed. Both of them were standing ramrod straight.

"I wasn't that bad, was I?" she asked, trying hard to keep the venom out of her voice.

Mark rolled his eyes. "I don't know. You looked good to me and Trevor didn't say anything before he started snapping off pictures. He would have said something if he didn't find your poses satisfactory. I don't think you did anything wrong, but this is crazy. We're already halfway through the morning and haven't even finished the second series of poses. The more time Alexander spends in his trailer, the less time you have to work on the coffee shop series. We weren't going to come back here tomorrow."

"Oh, yeah, tomorrow we are taking pictures in the subway, right?"

Mark nodded.

"Well, since Alexander's in the trailer, can I sit down for a few minutes?" Christina asked.

"Probably, since Trevor's in there, too."

Mark found her a folding chair and sat her down. Then to her immense surprise, he stood behind her and started rubbing her shoulders. And of course, every muscle in her body seized. Did he really have to do that in public?

"Don't tense up," Mark rebuked.

"But—"

"But nothing. I'm your agent and in a situation like this, I think you need something to help you relax."

Christina tried to do what Mark said. No one was looking at her funny or even really noticing what she and Mark were doing. Trevor's crew had all gotten themselves drinks and were mellowing on equipment carriers. Collin was nowhere to be seen, and neither was Laura. A few minutes after Trevor and Dominic went into the trailer; Mindy and the other makeup artist were shooed out.

Mindy came over to Mark and Christina with a frown the size of an upside-down row boat. "Whoa," she said, "That guy is really something else. Isn't he?"

"Did he say anything to you?" Mark asked.

"No," Mindy said, "but I was having a serious conversation with Sapphira about makeup and he comes trouncing in… argh!"

"Well, she's right over there," Mark said, pointing to Alexander's makeup artist. "And they might not be out of the trailer for a while. You might get more time to talk out here."

"Of course I was going to go talk to her," Mindy said, sounding offended that Mark pointed out something so obvious to her. "I just wanted to come see how Tina was holding up."

"I'm fine," Christina said earnestly. "I just hope Trevor isn't disappointed with me."

"Well, he's not out here explaining how you're the screw-up, now is he?" Mindy reminded her before saying to Mark snottily, "And Mark, if you want to be alone with Tina all you have to say is 'scram.' Okay? It's not like I'm her mother." Then she stalked away to go stand by Sapphira.

Mark kept on rubbing Christina's shoulders, but she was pointed toward the door to the trailer and couldn't stop worrying about what was happening inside. Was Alexander really being chewed out?

The minutes seemed to be going very slowly as the sun rose higher and higher in the sky. Soon it was past eleven and lunch was scheduled for noon. Mark got Christina a bottle of water and a couple of guys from Trevor's crew went for a cigarette break. It was eleven-thirty and the door still hadn't opened.

Finally, at a quarter to twelve, Trevor came out of the trailer. His eyes looked dark and angry. He came over to Christina and Mark. "Where's Collin?" he asked briskly.

"I don't know. He hasn't been back since you went in," Mark said.

"Whatever," Trevor said grouchily as he took his cell phone out of his pocket and started dialing. Then he moved away from them and over to his camera.

"Stay here," Mark said as he followed him.

Soon Trevor was surrounded by a small cluster of people, but Christina didn't see if he got Collin on the phone or not. Her attention was distracted by Alexander coming out of the trailer. He was wearing his own clothes and Dominic was following after him quickly with his cell phone pinned to his ear. It sounded like he was arranging for a car to pick them up. Alexander didn't look at Christina or anyone else as he left the set. He merely covered his eyes with a pair of dark sunglasses and disappeared behind the fans.

Christina would have loved to go have a chat with Dominic at that moment, but he was clearly not in the mood to hear how wrong he was. If Trevor looked like a thunder cloud when he came out of the trailer, Dominic looked like a typhoon—the kind with shrapnel in the wind. Despite a perfectly healthy Alexander walking in front of him, Dominic looked like he had just committed murder, infuriated beyond understanding. Christina would have loved to talk to him.

Mark came back over to Christina and explained, "Obviously, Alexander has refused to model."

"With me?" Christina asked carefully. "He doesn't mind doing the photoshoot, but just not with me, right?"

Mark ran a hand through his hair. It was obvious he desperately didn't want to answer that question. "That isn't what Trevor said, but the photoshoot has been put on hiatus for the time being. I guess we'll be back in the office tomorrow."

"Okay," Christina said slowly. She was still absorbing Alexander's rejection and deciding how she was going to deal with it. Once again, she thought she was in a situation where she would normally want to cry, but she didn't. Who cared if Alexander didn't like her? He was so bratty not even Dominic could reel him in.

"They were going to have a catered lunch here, but I think everyone would understand if you and I didn't stay for it. Can I take you for lunch and dinner?"

"You're just trying to make me feel better."

"Yeah, and if we don't get out of here quickly, I'm going to fail."

Chapter Fourteen

Up the Creek

Christina and Mark didn't tell Trevor where they were going for lunch, which was why they were so surprised when he showed up at their restaurant. He dropped himself into their booth, threw his bag across the bench and stretched his legs out so far Christina was positive he would trip a waitress… but maybe that was his plan.

"Hey kids," he said casually.

Mark gave him a funny look, but managed to be polite enough to ask without an attitude, "What are you doing here?"

Trevor shook his hand at Mark like he didn't realize he was interrupting a date. "I'm angry," he said simply.

"Of course you are. A whole morning wasted! What exactly happened with Alexander and Dominic anyway? Christina's convinced Alexander refused to pose with her," Mark explained.

Trevor nodded. "Sorry, Christina. Try not to take it personally. I don't think it had much to do with how you modeled or how you look."

"Then what was it about?"

Trevor shook his head. "I don't know. Considering how urgently Alexander wanted to leave the set, I'd say he simply had some other place else he wanted to be and he chose to say it was your bad modeling that was driving him away rather than take responsibility for what he was doing. Dominic certainly didn't want him to leave us in the lurch, hence the extended argument. You see, Alexander broke the conditions of his contact with Capier when he walked out today."

"How's Collin taking that?"

"I haven't been able to talk to him."

"Maybe Laura knows where he is," Mark said, retrieving his cell phone and finding Laura's profile. He programmed her number and put his phone to his ear. Within a few rings, Mark hung up. "Yeah, she's not answering either."

Trevor chuckled, "Lover's quarrel?"

"LOVER'S QUARREL?" Christina and Mark blurted at the exact same time.

"Huh?" Trevor said. "You didn't know? Collin and Laura have been together for a couple of years. They're a weird couple, eh?"

"Laura? With who? As far as I knew she was single!" Christina blurted.

Mark looked as perplexed as Christina. "Yeah, Trevor, Laura has been chasing me since I started working for Capier."

"What? Well, then I guess they broke up."

"I didn't know she was ever with Collin," Mark continued.

"Really? Back in the day, they were all over each other. The marriage issue must have finally done them in."

"What?"

"It's not an uncommon story. She wanted to get married—he kept putting her off. I knew they were fighting about it, but it's been a long time since I had a personal conversation with Collin."

Christina could hardly keep her astonishment in check. "But Mark and Collin are nothing like each other. How could she be interested in both of them? Collin's a…"

"Player?" Trevor supplied.

Actually, Christina would have said 'womanizer,' but she couldn't say something like that about her boss's boss, who hired a little nobody administrative assistant as a model? Saying even one word that might be interpreted as a slander was out of the question. She closed her mouth and waited for someone else to continue the conversation.

Luckily, Mark rescued her. "It's not so weird. Collin's unpredictable and Laura is a control freak. She probably got fed up with his crap and decided to go for someone who was more 'her type.' Me. Or maybe it was the other way around. Maybe Collin decided he didn't want to be with her for the same reason I did."

"What was that?" Trevor asked.

"I didn't want a girl I had to schedule time with."

"How ironic," Trevor said thoughtfully, taking his feet out of the aisle and putting them under the table. "That you should end up with Christina; a girl you not only had to schedule a date with, but also had to pay for."

Christina lifted her eyebrows and said frostily, "I thought we'd been through this."

"Sorry," Trevor said breaking from his reverie. "I didn't mean to insult you. Don't take what I said personally. I have a lot on my mind. I need to talk to Collin about the photoshoot because Alexander broke his contract. He says he won't come back to work until we have found a replacement for you, but I don't think we have time to find someone who suits Alexander. That is a tough job when you have all the time in the world. We need to have these shots done as soon as possible so we will have time to film a commercial before the end of the summer."

Christina sighed and looked away. She wanted to be helpful, but she didn't know how. She couldn't force Alexander to cooperate.

"So far, all of the shots Alexander has done for Capier he has done solo. Could it be that he really doesn't like sharing the stage?" Mark suggested.

"Maybe that's the problem. It's possible he doesn't think our project is a priority because he's not really the star. All the shots taken either focus on both him and Christina equally or they highlight Christina while he's left in the background. This phone is for women, so we need to show a woman using one which means he can't do the shoot without a female partner. Like I said, finding someone who can model with Alexander is challenging. When I saw Collin's pictures of you, Christina, I thought we had practically struck gold. You would look good with anybody... Which," Trevor said meaningfully, "is why I think it would be faster to replace Alexander than to replace you."

"With who?" Mark asked.

Trevor's eyes literally twinkled. "Mark," he said smoothly. "Do you remember the promise you made me in exchange for letting you live in my condo?"

"You don't mean—"

"Oh, but I do," Trevor said, fishing through his bag and withdrawing a magazine. "Christina, have a look at this."

Christina took the copy of *Teen Wish* and examined the cover. It was the prom issue.

Christina gaped.

Mark laughed when he saw it. "Where did you dig that up?"

"Dig it up? I keep a copy with me at all times," Trevor proclaimed noisily.

"Of course you do," Mark drawled. "How many years ago was that, anyway?"

"Five," Christina answered, looking at the date on the issue.

She flipped open the cover and found a younger Mark staring back at her. There he was on almost every other page sporting tuxedos and a fashionably messy hairstyle. He wasn't the main attraction, but merely an accessory to the girls who were modeling prom dresses. She could not believe how good he looked. Not only that but as she combed further into the issue, she found a picture of him that had been mounted on one of her school friend's walls. She remembered seeing the photo years and years ago and thinking he was hotter than the usual teen heartthrob, but naturally, completely untouchable, so not worth thinking about.

Christina turned to Mark and said, "This photo was up on my friend Shellie's wall when I was still in junior high."

"Really?" he asked, looking completely aghast.

"Yeah, really. Don't blush, Mark. You looked hot."

"Which is why I want him to take Alexander's place," Trevor said.

Christina stared at Trevor. "Can you do that?"

"Well, since I can't seem to get in touch with Collin, I guess I can do whatever I think is best. It would be a hassle to have to rebook all the locations and to rehire the temporary staff. The best thing is just to dress Mark up like Alexander—sans turtleneck of course—and to just get on with it." Trevor added, "Mark looks terrible in turtlenecks."

Christina couldn't believe what Trevor was suggesting. Switching Alexander for Mark would make the photoshoot fun, the opposite of hell on earth. Her pulse was already racing at the very idea.

"The best part is that Mark has modeled for me numerous times and I know he can deliver what Collin wants. And since I let him live in my place rent-free, he can't turn me down."

"Is that true?" Christina asked.

"Yes," Mark said slowly.

"So," Trevor said with a note of finality, "Eat up and we'll head back to the set. I want to finish the coffee shop pictures before the end of the day. I'll show Collin the pictures once we're finished. He'll like not having to dish out the big bucks for Alexander—especially when he's such a pain in the neck."

***

Trevor swapped Alexander's turtleneck for a white button-up-the-front shirt. "Mark's dark, see?" Trevor said, pulling a shirt out of the makeshift wardrobe. "So, we need a white shirt to contrast his coloring. He's not as tall as Alexander though, so he needs to wear a different size of trousers."

"Are you faking an English accent?" Christina suddenly asked.

Trevor smiled. "Not intentionally. I work with a lot of Brits. It rubs off." Then he jumped back into work. He thumbed through the spare clothes. "Hmm… nothing that would fit Mark."

Mark snorted. "Excuse me for being short."

"Well, what you're wearing isn't suitable. A cat has better fashion sense than you."

"You only think that because a cat runs around in the buff," Mark retorted and Christina silently agreed Trevor's modesty left something to be desired.

"You'll have to wear mine. Switch me," Trevor said, immediately unbuttoning his own black pants. He didn't even give Christina a chance to turn around. Apparently, he didn't mind if she saw his shiny black briefs.

Christina bolted out of the trailer. "Whoa," she said, leaning against the door after she clamped it shut.

"Hey," Mindy said coming up to her. "Trevor said we had to find a different shirt for you, too. What are you doing out here wearing the same thing?"

"Let's just give them a minute," Christina said, shaking her head.

Within half an hour, Christina and Mark were ready to go. Christina's wardrobe had been altered so that her blouse and coat were gone. Instead, she was wearing a black off-the-shoulder sweater and a scarf around her neck. Trevor liked the change because he said it made her more feminine. Plus, she had been wearing something similar in the initial pictures Collin took.

So, there was Christina up against the wall for a second time, but unlike the last time, it was Mark pushing her instead of Alexander. It was lucky... sort of. With the change, she was uncomfortable in a completely different way. She'd never seen Mark pretend before, and so she wasn't sure how much of his behavior was real or for the benefit of Trevor's camera. Were his eyes always dark, full of passion and awareness? Had his hand always felt confident when she held it before? Did the two of them always get along so well? Did he always look at her like with such awareness and did she just not see it before?

It was then Christina realized the flush on her cheeks wasn't one of her brain-induced rushes. It was quite the opposite——the real thing. Mark might not be able to tell when she was real, but Trevor did. He always shot off his camera shutter insanely at the most inopportune moments— right when Mark's gaze got too intense for Christina and she was about to look away. It made Christina blush even more furiously to have her heart exposed like that. But whenever she looked at the crew, it was just business as usual for them. They were selling phones. They didn't know it was her real heart on the line.

Trevor had a lot of poses up his figurative sleeve and he did rounds of more poses than she could count before he called it a day.

Christina was completely and totally drained. She stretched her arms and cocked her neck hoping to hear a satisfying crack.

"I don't feel like doing dinner tonight," Christina told Mark as he gave her a bottle of water. "I'm beat and by now, I'm probably too emotionally frazzled to appear in public."

"That's okay. I'm not really in the mood anymore either," he said shortly.

"All right then," Christina said, wondering about his dark mood. Maybe he didn't really want to pose after all. "I'm going to change."

Christina turned to go into the trailer and was surprised to see Mark walking behind her. She peeked around at him a couple of times and looked at him meaningfully trying to communicate to him that she wanted to go alone because she was obviously going to change into her street clothes. But he didn't seem to catch the hint and kept right on following her.

At the door, she stopped, "Mark I..."

Mark reached past her and opened the door. "After you," he said, steering her into the trailer.

Christina felt lost as she stumbled into the empty trailer. What did he need to talk to her about that couldn't wait until after she had taken her wretched wig off? Regardless, she couldn't wait to start getting comfortable. Whatever. If he wanted to watch, it wouldn't be the first time.

"What is it?" she asked him as she stepped up to her dressing table and started unscrewing the backs of her earrings. She set them on the table as Mark gradually came up behind her and started rubbing her shoulders.

"You're tired, aren't you?" he whispered as he drew back the curtain of her hair and began kissing her ear.

Christina could see their reflection in the mirror as he worked his way down her neck. His kisses were soft and his breath warm. Christina's legs felt wobbly; she didn't know if she could keep standing. One of his hands went to the back of her throat and tugged her scarf free. He wrapped it between his fingers, to keep it from falling. Christina felt so weak she couldn't keep her eyes open. But even as his arms encircled her and he pulled her around to face him, somehow she couldn't lose sight of where they were.

"Mark," she sighed. "Do you really think this is a good place? What if someone walks in on us?"

His dark eyes locked on hers and he asked roughly, "Don't you want me to touch you?" He kissed her again and she could sense his desperation for her. It was in every one of his motions.

She didn't know what to do. She felt like such a tramp. How could she make out with her boss at work? It seemed so sleazy, except for the pounding of her heart. She was so excited by him that she didn't know if she could push him away.

Knock! Knock! Knock!

Christina thrust Mark off her and quickly turned around to continue taking off her jewelry. She was just in time because Trevor and Mindy came crashing into the trailer talking about how great work had been that day. Christina was beet-red, but she acted as if nothing happened. She was pretty sure they hadn't seen anything, but when she looked at Mark... she saw she had offended him.

He stalked behind a Chinese screen to change his clothing and when he emerged, he didn't look the least bit happier. Before he left the trailer entirely, he gave Christina a look that was both disappointed and extremely frustrated.

Chapter Fifteen

A Makeover for the Ages

Christina eyed Mark on the other side of the set. There was quite the bustle of people coming and going with equipment and extension cords. The talk outside the trailer was all business.

The second photoshoot was scheduled for one o'clock in the morning; technically, two days later. The pictures were to be taken in the subway, and since they were to include pictures of the train, they needed to be taken after hours.

Christina asked Mark if she should come to work the day before the shoot, but Mark said there was no need. He wasn't going to work that morning either. Apparently, he simply took over Alexander's contract, with the exception of pay. Mark wasn't worth as much as Alexander. She overheard Trevor offering him less than a quarter of what they were going to pay Alexander. Trevor apologized for the cut, but Mark shook his head and said it was part of their agreement that he would model for Trevor whenever he needed him, so it was fine. He laughed and said he was happy Trevor wasn't considering him a complete freebie.

Then he came back to Christina. His bad mood seemed to have evaporated. It was one of the tricks of a PR officer. He could turn it on and turn it off. "Sorry Christina," he said. "I'd like to take you to my place to rest tonight, but Trevor is going to be there as soon as he finishes here, so we wouldn't have any privacy."

"That's okay," Christina said smiling, but she couldn't help but wonder what Mark was thinking. She hadn't stayed over at his place once. Why would she start when she was so bleeding tired? "I'm just going to go home and have a hot bath, and I'll see you in the subway tomorrow night, okay?" Then she started walking away.

"Wait," Mark said, grabbing her arm. "Can I see you tomorrow? We have the whole day off."

Christina laughed. "Maybe *you* have the whole day off. Since I don't have to come into work, Mindy booked me. She was really worried she wouldn't have enough time to doll me up for the subway shots because I wouldn't get home from work until six, but now that I'm free, I'm sure she's figured out an entire day of soaking and steaming. Hopefully, I'll come out looking smooth," Christina said with a wink.

"Can't you make a little time?"

"Maybe in the morning," Christina said quietly. He was certainly persistent.

"What time?" Mark asked.

"I don't know—early."

"I'll be over early then." He kissed her on the cheek and let her go.

Christina stumbled away to find Mindy since they were supposed to be driving home together, but she couldn't get his expression out of her head. What was it about glamorous Tina that never failed to captivate Mark's interest? No matter what he said, he always acted differently toward her when she was dressed up like Tina. It was clear he was far more attracted to her... and that stung.

***

The next morning, Christina's nose felt itchy. She scratched it and rolled onto her stomach. Then the itch moved to her ear. She scratched that, too. Then the side of her neck, her elbow, the back of her hand, and then her neck again. Fed up, she sat up and scratched everything.

"Good morning, Tina," a deep voice whispered.

Christina woke herself up the rest of the way and saw Mark sitting on the edge of her bed. He was holding a long white feather. He'd been tickling her with it.

She looked at the clock and saw not only a bra hanging over the nightstand, but also the time—seven... am. She snatched the bra and shoved it under her pillow. "Mark, what are you doing here?"

"You said early," he said, leaning back on his elbows.

"Yeah, early. Couldn't you have called?" she asked as she jumped up to find any other offending pieces of clothing she might have left lying around. "Or at least knocked before you came into my *bedroom*?"

"But I wanted to come over *before* you woke up. You look so cute when you sleep," he teased.

"Did Mindy let you in?"

"She's nice, isn't she?"

Christina stood there in her pajamas and stared at him. After his behavior yesterday, she would have expected to find him a wolf today—predatory and hungry—for a lack of better words. But instead, he was laughing and chummy. He had even dropped the feather, so there wasn't the faintest hint of a forthcoming seduction scene. It felt like their fiery kiss in the trailer the day before hadn't happened.

Christina snatched her blue moon housecoat off the hook and put it on. She ruffled her short hair until it practically stood up on end. "Would you like something to eat?" she asked.

"Couldn't I take you out for breakfast again?" he invited.

"No," Christina said, she opened the door to her bedroom and went out into the kitchen. "I have to get dressed up later and I'm not doing it twice when I'm this tired. I'm making eggs on toast for myself. Would you like me to make some for you, too?" Christina opened the fridge and started pulling out ingredients. There wasn't much there that belonged to her.

Mark followed her into the kitchen and started looking in the cupboards for a frying pan. He found one and put it on the burner for her. "Tell you what, since I was so inconsiderate, why don't I cook for you? You said you wanted eggs on toast? I'll make them for you. You sit down and I'll do all the work."

He led her toward the table and Christina dropped herself into one of the chairs.

Mark opened the fridge and found some orange juice. He was about to pour a glass when Christina stopped him. "Don't drink that!" Christina said urgently, stopping him in mid-pour.

"Why?" he questioned, confused.

"That's Mindy's. I didn't buy it."

"You and Mindy don't buy groceries together?"

"No," Christina said, shaking her head. "She had some bad experiences with her last roommate and so she said she wanted to buy things separately. I bought the milk, so you can have that."

"I was pouring this *for you*, not me," he said, returning the orange juice to the fridge and taking out the milk. The way he said 'for you' made Christina's heart skip. He brought her the milk and turned back to the stove where he started cracking eggs into a bowl. "You know," he said lazily. "I was thinking you never got to try my stir fry."

"No, I didn't. Laura and Dominic interrupted us."

"Yeah," he said, deliberately keeping his back to Christina. "I feel like whenever we get a few minutes alone together we're interrupted by someone. Yesterday, it was Mindy and Trevor; both in the trailer and when I took you out for lunch. It feels like there's always someone in line who wants you, wants me, or wants both of us. I'm starting to get fed up."

"It does seem like we're suffering from some rotten luck," Christina admitted. "I'm sorry," she said, looking dreamily through the kitchen window out onto the sun-dappled parking lot. "And it doesn't look like it's going to let up anytime soon. We still have two more photo sessions, and then the wrap-up party. We're going to some club, aren't we?"

"Yeah," he answered quietly.

Christina didn't catch the frustration in his voice and continued, "Then we'll both be back at our desks working. It's kind of hard to be a couple at work, isn't it?"

Mark turned around and looked squarely at Christina as the eggs crackled in the frying pan behind him, "Maybe we won't be back at our desks. At least, I might not be."

"Why not?"

"Trevor found a job for me," Mark admitted.

Christina giggled. "Working as a model?"

"No," Mark said, looking uncomfortable. "It's a job in public relations. Trevor has been after me to take it since he got back. The offer was pretty impressive."

The reason for Mark's discomfort was becoming clear to Christina. "It's not here, is it?" she asked.

"No, it's in London. That's why I don't want to take it. To me, it looks like just one more obstacle. I want to be with you, but… it pays a lot more money and I'd be the director of the public relations department instead of just an officer. So, I'm tempted."

"Are you asking me what I think?" Christina asked, taking a sip of milk.

"Well," Mark said. "You *are* my girlfriend. You deserve to have your say before I make my decision. I'd like to hear your opinion."

Christina sat quietly for a second, thinking. Mark was leaning against the counter examining her expression and waiting for her reply.

It was going to tear her apart to say 'good-bye' to him, but she couldn't stop thinking about their relationship. It always felt like he liked *Tina* far more than *Christina*, and she couldn't tie him down if the one he liked wasn't her true self. She had always thought he was more than she could handle. Why would a guy like him want to be with a plain-Jane girl like her?

"Mark," she said quietly. "It sounds like a great opportunity. I think you should probably take it."

"You don't want me to stay?" he asked as he turned around and started scrambling the eggs crossly.

"Of course I want you to stay, but I also don't want to hold you back. You know, it's a delicate balance, but…"

"But what?"

"But," Christina swallowed hard and braced herself for what she was about to say. "I was never really good enough for you to begin with. You're incredible, fascinating, and you have it all together and I… just pretend. You deserve someone who doesn't need to dress up to get your attention."

"Is that how you really feel? Is that how I make you feel?" he asked. His voice was tight and dry.

She'd screwed up. He didn't take it as a compliment at all. What could she say? She felt tortured. She had to come up with a way to smooth everything over as quickly as possible, but no ideas were coming.

When she didn't answer him, Mark turned around and approached her. "You know, sometimes I feel like my feelings are too close to the surface. Maybe I leave my face too open and you read exactly what I think and feel—and then you say exactly the right thing to either excite me into ecstasy or to twist the knife that much deeper. Are you doing it intentionally? What exactly do you want from me?"

"I don't know what you're talking about! I'm not like that," Christina cried.

"Really? What about yesterday during the shoot? Trevor wouldn't have cared if we kissed on the set, while he was taking pictures of us. No one would have cared, but you kept on turning your face away over and over again."

"I didn't do it to insult you or to push you away. I thought you weren't serious and you were just hamming it up for the shoot."

"And then in the trailer? I fell on my face when you pushed me away," he accused.

"But Mindy and Trevor came in! It wouldn't have been professional!"

Mark stared at her wide-eyed. "Are you really that straight-laced? Give me a break. You had no problem with public displays of affection when you worked as an escort. Why be squeamish now? Besides, it was Trevor and Mindy. I can't even think of two people who would have cared less if they caught us kissing."

Christina exhaled heavily. "I'm sorry Mark, but I keep telling you that I'm not really experienced when it comes to that sort of thing. Apparently, I make stupid mistakes. I honestly wasn't trying to hurt your feelings. I'm not like that."

"Well, I've been trying very hard to figure out who you are, Christina. Sometimes, you're so hot it seems impossible a woman like you exists and sometimes you are the girl-next-door to a T."

"I *am* the girl-next-door," Christina said sorrowfully. That was the truth and she might as well get it out in the open. He might as well know who he was dealing with.

"Bull!" Mark accused. "If that was all there was to you then it would be impossible for you to pull off being Tina. Maybe you're not a little girl anymore and you don't want to deal with the fact that you can be a skilled man-eater."

"But you are never attracted to me when I'm not dressed like Tina!" Christina wailed, finally saying exactly what was on her mind. "You're always trying to get me to go out with you while dressed like her."

"For your information, it's not just how you look. It's how you act. You can think I'm shallow if you like, but I promise, it's not just the long hair and additional curves. You act flirty. It's cute."

Christina bit her lip. She was listening carefully to what he had to say, but her vision got blurry when she realized that what she'd believed all along was true. He did like her better as Tina.

"You'd better go," she said quietly. "Thank you for making me breakfast." Then she got up and headed towards her bedroom.

"Wait," Mark said, grabbing her arm.

"Don't say anything else, Mark," she said, jerking her arm free. "Look, everything is cool between us, but if we keep talking it won't stay that way and we need to work together tonight. So, just consider this a breather and I'll see you tonight. Okay?"

"Okay," he said and made his way to the door. Apparently, he understood as well as she did their need to get along for the sake of the campaign.

Christina listened to him put on his shoes and go out the door. She heard his footsteps down the hallway and she even heard him open the door to the stairs. What if it was the last time he came and the last time he left? The thought was too much for Christina.

She'd always felt like Mark was too good for her. She wasn't the kind of girl who could win a guy like him, was she? Her conversation with him had done two things. First, it had made her miserable. Second, it let her know how she could not only get Mark but also how she could make him happy. Did she like him bad enough to make the sacrifice? To give up being Christina?

When her determination became concrete, she got up and went into Mindy's bedroom. She wouldn't be able to go through with her plan without Mindy's help.

After Christina explained, Mindy laughed. "Are you sure you want to do this? It's sort of intense, and it could end badly."

"I want to," Christina said boldly, rubbing the tension out of her shoulders. "I want to see if he means what he says. If he's really that far gone over Tina, then let's see how far he'll go if we give her to him."

"Are you trying to drive the man insane?"

"Maybe."

Mindy shrugged her shoulders. "And what about Christina? What will happen to her?"

"She's me. She'll always be me, so it won't matter if I give this a try," Christina said stiffly.

"If that's how you feel, then I'll help you, but today is going to be brutal. Prepare yourself!" Mindy grabbed her cell phone and started making calls.

Chapter Sixteen

Devilish Laugh

The photoshoot in the subway was pretty fun. After the previous photoshoot, Christina didn't believe Trevor could have more poses up his sleeve, but miraculously, he did. He did these crazy shots with Christina standing on one platform while Mark stood on the opposite one and the train sped between them. At least, that was what Trevor said they would look like once he was finished with them.

Christina and Mark spoke briefly before Trevor started taking pictures.

"How are you feeling?" Mark asked gently.

Christina looked him up and down. He was wearing the same clothes he had worn for the shoot the day before. So was she. He still looked absolutely mouth-watering and Christina was positive she was right to do what she could to try to win Mark even though her shoulders ached. Essentially, she'd worked from early morning and all day to try to make herself ready—not for the photoshoot—for him. He couldn't even see everything she'd done since she was wearing the wig. Some of it was visible anyway, but it didn't seem like he noticed. Well, he *would* notice.

She pouted her lips and glanced at his face again before returning to her water. "It's a little cold down here," she said, touching her bare shoulder with her fingertips.

"Do you want a coat?" he asked considerately.

"No," she said, even though she had goosebumps. "We have to get to work. Are you ready?" The playful look she gave him wasn't lost on him as he joined her in front of the camera lens.

For these shots, they weren't posed so closely together and very few of the shots required Mark and Christina to touch each other. She had to use every ounce of her charisma to make herself blush like she was the luckiest girl in the world when she wanted to stare Mark down like a stalker.

By the end of the shoot, Trevor was congratulating both of them on a hard day's work. He took fewer shots than he had the day before. "I'm pretty sure I got what I wanted," he said lightly, but Christina could tell he was about to fall on his face from sheer exhaustion.

She bit her lip to make it look plumper and touched Trevor on the shoulder. "Are you feeling alright?" she asked in her most delicate little-girl voice.

"Yeah," he said, forcing himself to perk up. "I just had a really long meeting with Collin this afternoon and I'm fried."

"He didn't get out of it until it was time to start setting up here," Mark said between tight lips. "So, we're finished?"

"We're finished," Trevor yawned. "You two can get changed."

Christina took Mark's hand and led him up the escalator. Their trailer was above ground. She slid her arm around his waist and, by doing so, practically got into his coat with him.

"So, we didn't break up this afternoon?" Mark asked, sounding like something was still wrong.

"Did you think we had?" she asked, looking deeply into his eyes.

"Well, I made you sad… or mad… or…" Mark stuttered. He couldn't help it; Christina was playing with his hair and intentionally blowing in his ear.

"Bad?" she asked quietly. Then she stepped off the escalator. She couldn't believe it when he stumbled. "Come on," she said, pulling on his hand. "I want to get changed."

When they got into the trailer, Christina got behind the Chinese screen and started stripping. She was very uncomfortable, but she pulled it off as best she could. She draped her shirt over the edge and started talking.

"Mark, we may have had an argument this morning, but that's all in the past now. I thought about what you said and I think you have a good point."

"Do you?"

"Yeah," she said, while she zipped up a pair of Mindy's black pants. "A girl wants to be treated like a princess, so why shouldn't she look like one if that's what she wants?" Christina slipped a shiny black tank top over her head. "You know?" she said as she came out from behind the screen.

Mark reached for her, but she walked right past him to her dressing table. "I want to take off my wig," she said.

"Ah, but of course," Mark said, like at least something she said was starting to make sense. He started unlacing his boots.

Christina had to be very careful as she took off her wig. She didn't want to upset what was underneath. Of all the things Christina had done that afternoon to try to get ready to be Tina all the time, one of them had been the hardest. She had gotten extensions. When she took off her wig, she had long straight honey-colored strands that were really attached to her head. Mark liked long hair, so she was giving him long hair. She picked up a brush and started smoothing it.

"Is that another wig?" Mark asked. He had gotten up and was standing beside her.

"No. This is my hair now. What do you think?"

"It looks good," Mark said, twirling a strand between his fingers. His eyebrows were pulled together and he was clearly confused.

Christina shrugged her shoulders like she didn't care what he thought and started putting on her jewelry. She put on two silver hoop earrings, thick silver rings, and three hoop bracelets. Then she grabbed a little red cardigan and put it on to cover her shoulders.

"Are you going to get changed?" she asked looking at his clothes. "Mindy left already, so I was hoping you could give me a ride home."

"What are you playing at?" he asked, looking at her like he was more worried about her than enchanted.

"I told you already. You said you liked the way I looked when I dressed up, so I'm trying it out, okay? Does it make you like me better to see me dressed like this?"

"So, this is for my benefit?"

"It's for mine," she said briefly. She was about to say more, when Mark suddenly bent down and kissed her. His hands were all over her and his lips and breath were so hot. It was everything she wanted. She needed him to feel the same way about her that she felt about him. His hands were on her back and he crushed the fabric of her shirt in his fists. Her knees were buckling. She felt so weak; like she might faint or fall on the floor. The trailer around them was becoming dark.

In the end, she had to pull away from him before she blacked out.

"What's wrong?"

Christina didn't know what to say, so she stumbled over to her bag and took out her shoes. "You're really hot," she said. "It's sort of too much for me right now. I think I need to get some air. We can pick up here after I've got control of myself."

"That's supposed to be my line after I do something uncalled for and you shove me off," Mark said as he reached for her again.

"I'll just be a minute," she said, evading him.

"Wait," Mark begged as she slipped out of the trailer and stood on the empty city street.

"Just two breaths," she promised. Then she closed the door between them. It delighted her that he looked disappointed.

Christina took two heavy breaths, but she didn't feel refreshed. What was she going to do? She wasn't confident she could keep herself conscious and if she couldn't even kiss him for thirty seconds, how was she going to fare when they got further along? And he was so intense. She'd had better control of the situation on New Year's Eve.

She lazily made her way down the three steps that led to the trailer, thinking.

"Tina, is that you?" a voice suddenly came out of the darkness.

Christina's head swung around. "Who's there?"

"Nothing to fear," the smooth voice continued as Dominic stepped into the light of the trailer. "It's just me."

"What do you want?" she asked crossly.

"I wanted to thank you for your help. My sister is all set up now, so there is nothing to worry about."

"She's not with Mark… or Trevor," Christina squeaked.

"If only either of those guys had anything to do with the *real* plan," he drawled as he took a slow drag from his cigarette. He looked ghastly in the weird yellow light from the trailer. His hair and skin were so pale and his eyes shone out through his red glasses. "She was only trying to get Collin to the altar and so now that she's won him, I'm finally free."

"Goody for you," Christina said sarcastically. She didn't care two straws if Dominic owed Laura favors. "When's the wedding?"

"It was yesterday. I think they'll announce it at your wrap-up party."

"Oh? Really? And why are you here now? Is Alexander bummed about missing out on the shoot?"

"Why would he be bummed about that? Like he cares if he blows off Capier! In his mind he was only doing it as a favor to Laura."

"And in your mind?" Christina asked, thinking of Dominic's face when Alexander walked off the set.

"They were important clients," he admitted wearily. "Any paycheck is better than none, which is where he's headed."

"And you?" Christina asked suspiciously. "Did you decide to blow him off?"

"Soon, Tina, soon. It won't be long now before he isn't offered anything new. He ran off the set. News gets around fast, and it's very bad business to walk out because of a temper tantrum. He already has a bad reputation and now I suppose it's going to get worse. I won't have anything to book if he keeps this up. So, whether I drop him or not is unimportant."

"So, what about your career? Alexander acted like he was your full-time job. If you don't have him, what do you plan to do?" Christina asked suspiciously.

Dominic seemed to slither as he moved toward her. "I'll have to scout new talent of course."

"So, you want to be my agent?" she asked, her eyes wide.

"I really think you have potential."

"Do you?"

"I want to make you an offer."

"What sort of offer?" Christina asked sceptically.

"I have a job for you working as a fashion model. It'll last about four months and then we'll see if we can find you something new after that."

"Where is it?"

"London," he said and the word seemed to hang in the air like a glowing moon between them.

"Oh crap," Christina said out loud. She couldn't help thinking about what Mark had told her that afternoon about moving to London for a job in public relations. Christina put her hand to her forehead. If the job offer wasn't just some lame trick of Dominic's than it was her way to go with Mark to London legitimately. Mark could take his great job offer and she could take hers. They could still see each other while not being in anyone's way. She was sorely tempted. She really didn't want to let Mark go, but she didn't know what she could offer him that would make him want to stay.

"Are you tempted just because of the location?" Dominic asked coyly. "How curious!"

"I'll have to think about it," Christina said quietly.

"That's all? You just need to move to London? You don't care what the pay is, or what the job will be like, what hours you'll work, what clothes you'll wear, or anything? All that matters to you is that you'll live in London."

Christina rolled her eyes. "Don't pick up on things so quickly," she said wretchedly. "Or if you do, at least have the grace not to talk about them out loud. But now that you're mentioning it, I do have one question."

"And that question is?" Dominic asked as he flicked away his cigarette.

"What's the catch?"

"What catch?"

"There has to be something you want me to do for you in exchange for this marvelous opportunity. You'd better tell me that part before we go any further."

Dominic hesitated before he said sweetly, "It's nothing really. A token."

Christina waited for him to finish with her hands on her hips. She drummed her fingers on her hip bone.

"Oh, don't be so grouchy!" Dominic accused as he came right in front of her so that her toes on the step above brushed his shins. He took off his sunglasses and showed her the purple circles under his eyes. "I just want to make up with you. You said those horrible things about me. I've been miserable ever since we weren't friends."

"Okay, then," she said, feeling sorry for him. "I accept your apology."

"I didn't apologize," he said, squinting. "Yet," he said and then without warning his hands were gripping her cheeks and his mouth was on hers.

Christina didn't have a chance to do anything; not to push him off, not to bite him, not to scream, or do anything else before a harsh voice interrupted them.

"Tina!" Mark barked from the trailer door.

Dominic pulled off her, but quickly maneuvered Christina into a sideways hug so that her arms were pinned to her sides.

"Let go of me!" she yelled, but Dominic did no such thing.

He simply answered Mark by saying, "You're interrupting."

"Am I?" Mark said with his eyebrows arched.

"Mark! Help me!" Christina screamed. Dominic wasn't telling go.

Mark took a deep breath and came down the steps. "Let go of her, Dominic."

"Or what?" Dominic asked, holding tight to Christina while she struggled.

"I hate you," Mark said weakly, and Christina wasn't sure if he was talking to her or Dominic.

Then Mark punched Dominic squarely on the jaw. He let go of Christina and fell back onto the pavement.

"Leave her alone," Mark said, taking Christina's hand and striding quickly away from the trailer.

"Not on your life," Dominic yelled, still lying flat on his back. "She's going to be my new model."

Mark whipped around and looked Christina in the eye. "Is that what you two were talking about?"

Christina nodded. She was stuck, but if she lied it would be worse.

Mark looked incredulous, but he gripped her hand tighter and hurried her toward his car. He opened the door for her and even helped her inside.

He got behind the wheel and pushed the button so all the doors locked automatically. "He was attacking you, right?"

"Yes," Christina said. "But he wasn't lying about the job. He offered me one."

"And you? Did you want to take it?"

Christina was about to answer when Mark interrupted her, "So, I take that P.R. job and move to London and you become Dominic's new feature model, is that it? No hard feelings between us because we'll break up for the sake of my job and then you can do whatever you want."

"The job he offered me was in London. I listened to him because I want to be with you," she squealed. She had to get the truth out before he exploded.

"And the only way you can think of to get us to be together is to whore yourself off to Dominic? Why not just ask me if you can come with me? You're my assistant, whether we're lovers or not. I'd still have asked you to come. You are a great assistant."

"And that's what you love about Christina? That she's a great assistant?"

"What's that supposed to mean?"

"You know what, Mark?" Christina yelled, as tears formed in her eyes. "Forget about me. You wanted me to be Tina, so I became her. If you take me to London, then you want me to be Christina, so you'll have an assistant. Don't you understand? I do not have the energy to be both people! I am either Tina or Christina. If I'm Christina, then you go to London by yourself because she would never go that far for a man who would never love her properly. She'd stay and work at Capier for a different P.R. officer."

"And if you're Tina?" Mark asked quickly.

"I don't know," Christina said thoughtfully. "She's the kind of girl who makes big demands and gets what she wants. She won't come just to be your girlfriend, and she'd make a mess of your office because she'd flirt with everyone. If you want her to come, you'll have to make her a pretty impressive offer."

"What kind of offer?"

Christina frowned and risking everything, she said, "It would have to be big. You'd have to promise to love her forever. You know, give her something worth giving up her boring self for and worth giving up her flirtatious self for. You have to make it worth her giving everything for you. Big."

Mark started the engine and turned on the headlights. "And you'd come to London with me?"

Christina nodded her head in the darkness.

"What about Dominic?"

"I don't think he's going to be easy to get rid of. I never dreamed he would go that far for me."

Mark smirked in the darkness and threw his car into reverse. "I told you," he said sharply. "Tina makes guys want to do that."

Chapter Seventeen

Breaking it up

"How did it go?" Mindy asked Christina when she stepped into their apartment very late that night.

"Badly," Christina said as she dropped her keys, bag and shoes in the entryway. She came into the living room and threw herself into Mindy's recliner. "I hate everyone," Christina said expressionlessly, even though that wasn't how she was feeling.

"Well, I warned you," Mindy said, shrugging in her more-experienced-than-you manner. She leaned forward and asked, "So, what's the verdict? Do you get Mark, like you wanted?"

"I'm not sure I want him anymore. Did I tell you that he got offered a job in London?"

"No," Mindy gasped. "Bloody Hell! Is that what this is about? You were trying to get him to stay?"

"Not exactly. I was trying to get him to like me properly, but you were right about that, too. He's never going to like me the way I want him to. Now I'm so confused about who I am, I'm not sure I can salvage things with Mark even if he doesn't go anywhere."

"You might not be able to," Mindy conceded. "Loads of relationships fail."

"I just thought he was so intelligent, so good looking and so everything I ever wanted in a guy that I couldn't stand for him to only like me half-way. What is it about stupid men that make them lose their minds over girls like you or Tina?"

"I am NOT like Tina," Mindy snapped, getting up and coming over to Christina. "I am not like you when I work as an escort."

"But you're the one who taught me to be like that!"

"Right, but that's because I knew that style would work for you. You come off like an innocent little girl who is discovering love for the first time because, Christina, that's what you are! In case you hadn't clued in, that's why you are such a good choice for your company's ad campaign. And that's why it works so well for Mark to be your partner for it—because it's all real. Except now you're discovering that love can be a brat, too." Mindy paused and took a deep breath. "And that is why I'm not like you. I already know. I was a little girl once too, but I've been disappointed too many times to look innocent."

Christina frowned. What Mindy was saying made a lot of sense. A lot more sense than she would have liked. If it was true, then she wouldn't be able to make a success of the job Dominic offered her, even if she wanted to take it, because that would require someone good at modeling. Or at least it required someone who actually *wanted* to be a model, which she didn't.

"All right," Christina admitted, putting a weary hand to her forehead. "What can I do to cope with this?"

Mindy settled down a little and dropped herself back down onto the couch. "I guess that all depends on how badly things went. Did you break up with him?"

"No."

"Did he break up with you?"

"No," Christina said, feeling a little better. At least things hadn't deteriorated that far.

Then Mindy asked the crucial question, "Do you want to break up with him?"

Christina winced. Then she said miserably, "I can't see how I can straighten this out and get the kind of love affair I want and my pride is bruised. He's thinking about how far he's willing to go for me... for Tina. He didn't give me an answer, and even if he does, I'm not sure I want to hear it."

"So, what are you going to do?"

Christina thought about it for a second, but if she really was going to break up with him than the answer was pretty clear. "First, I need to swallow my feelings and make it through this last photoshoot."

"Correct," Mindy said approvingly. "It really wouldn't look good on me, you, Mark, Trevor or Collin if you ran squealing at this point. You would look worse than Alexander, especially since this is your first time modeling."

"Then I need to quit my job working as Mark's assistant," Christina continued.

"Are you sure you're okay with that?" Mindy asked. "I mean, you worked so hard to get an honest job."

"Well, if I'm breaking up with him then I can't keep working for him. After I make it through the photoshoot I won't be able to work with him for one more day."

"I guess if that's how you feel," she mumbled.

"Come on, Mindy," Christina pleaded. "If you've been hurt, you have to know how important it is to get away from the person who has hurt you."

"I didn't disagree with you," Mindy defended.

"Good. Then I need to get on a bus to visit my parents. Then I'll figure out what to do from there."

"What about the wrap-up party?"

"What about it?"

"Don't you need to go?" Mindy asked.

"Maybe," Christina considered. "But don't I just have to show up, order a drink, pour it onto a plant, congratulate Collin, and then head for the door?"

Mindy bit her lip, "What if *I'm* not comfortable with that?"

Christina shook her head, "Why should you care?"

"During this whole thing, you have been Tina when dealing with the crew and I don't want you to leave sniveling. You should have perfect PR during this whole thing no matter what you want to do next. Besides, I want to do a favor for you because you got me that job doing your makeup."

"What are you talking about?"

"It'll be your last night dressed up like Tina, right?"

"I don't know," Christina said, fingering her false hair. "I spent so much money on these extensions it seems stupid to get rid of them."

"It'll be your last night with Mark, then?"

"Yes," Christina choked. She hadn't said she was going to break up with Mark, quit her job, and run for the hills, but before she finished talking she knew that's what she was going to do.

"Then, let's do it with style."

"It'll have to be in my innocent style then because I don't know if I can pull off your experienced one," Christina said, pinching her nose between her eyes.

"Escort style," Mindy corrected.

Christina looked up. At once she knew what Mindy was talking about. "Mindy, you are an absolute angel!"

***

The final photo session was to take place in Collin's office. They dressed the room up like a woman's office. The general idea was that it was supposed to be Tina's office and Mark was coming to visit her. They did quite a few shots with him peeking around the door. Then they did some with her sitting on the desk with her cute cell phone. All the pictures included shots of the cell phone, but these didn't have Mark in them at all. They were just her and the phone. Christina was starting to get quite attached to it. She was thinking of buying one when they came on sale.

The last shots were a lot easier for Christina. Maybe it was because she'd been doing it for the past two days or maybe it was because Mark wasn't as intense as he'd been in the past. He made his face look the way Trevor wanted, but other than that; he was pretty hands-off about the whole thing.

When they were finished, the entire crew planned to go out to a club. Since clean-up took a couple of hours, everyone wasn't ready to go until around eight. Christina and Mark helped too since there was so much work to do.

Right before they were set to leave, Mindy plopped Christina into her makeup chair and did her makeup one last time.

"Don't think too much about what we're doing tonight," she advised as she applied Christina's blush. "Just have a good time."

"I'll try," Christina said, finally allowing herself to feel mournful. Nothing Mark had said or done that day had convinced her she was making the wrong decision. He was polite and courteous, but not remarkable. Lucky for him, he didn't look smug. If he had Christina would have looked forward to twisting the knife. Instead, he just looked indifferent. Christina could never tell how he was feeling anyway.

After Mindy was finished, the two girls went and put on their clubbing gear. Mindy wore a gold-colored top and black pants. She looked like a panther. Christina wore a light green dress that gathered over one shoulder and hung loosely over the other. Little beads were sewn artfully across it like a fairy had lost her balance over Christina's head and dropped stars all over her. As she looked into the mirror in the bathroom, she thought she looked better than she'd ever looked for a date before. Even though she was dressed like Tina, she could still see herself peeking out through the facade.

When she and Mindy came out of the bathroom, Mark was waiting for them. To Christina, his expression was unfathomable, but Mindy seemed to think something when she saw him. If anything, it was as though Mindy understood something Christina did not.

"You look nice," he said to Christina as he took her arm and led her toward the elevator.

Mindy hung outside as the doors closed, her feet firmly planted on the carpet.

"Wait, Mindy. Aren't you coming too?" Christina called.

"Go on without me. I'll catch a ride with Trevor," she said and the elevator doors closed between them.

Then she and Mark were alone in the elevator as it went down. The air seemed too hot to Christina even though the building was air-conditioned. She felt like she was going to suffocate and the seconds seemed to be ticking backward. Would she ever get out?

"We need to talk," Mark said at last.

"Okay," Christina said. Her voice was like a drop of water falling into a sea, it could barely be heard.

"Do you want to blow off this party and come over to my place?"

"You kill me," Christina said sarcastically.

"We need to talk and we can't do it there. It'll be too noisy."

"Is that the Mark I know talking? It doesn't seem like it. You see, the Mark I know wouldn't skip out on a company event to be with his girlfriend. He wouldn't even turn away a second girl when he's already on a date if she's part of the institution. Both his and his lover's wants are completely unimportant compared to his professional obligations."

"Really?"

"Yup," she said, not sounding near chipper enough for the use of the word. "Besides, I can't ditch. I promised Mindy I would be there. She really wants to be a makeup artist and it'll make her look bad if I don't show up. I think she's planning on greasing some wheels tonight."

"Who would be there to grease?" Mark asked incredulously.

"Trevor and Collin," Christina answered smoothly. "She's got to try her best, and I'm her cousin. I can't leave her in the lurch. I love her."

Just then the elevator opened and Christina and Mark stepped out.

"We can talk in the car," Christina offered as she hurried ahead of him to the front doors of the building.

"You want to talk about London in the car?" Mark asked, rushing after her.

"I'm not going to London. I haven't heard from Dominic since last night and if I do, I'll let him outright I'm not going with him. I'd make a crappy model. My emotions are way too likely to get involved and I'd just get hurt over and over again. No thanks."

"What about me?" Mark asked, grabbing both her shoulders and forcing her to face him.

"Oh yeah," Christina said, trying to act like she was forgetting the smallest of details. "I was going to tell you. I quit. I won't be coming into work on Monday."

"Why?" Mark said, seeking her eyes in the most sincere way.

"Because," she said, trying to match his sincerity with venom. "We're breaking up."

"Because of London?"

"No," Christina said licking her lips. "Because I won't follow you there just to be your assistant."

"You already said that."

"And because," she continued. "It's impossible for me to be what you want."

"I'll tell you what I want."

"I'm not interested," she said, fighting off his hands and walking past him.

"What about what I don't want? Cause I don't want Tina!" he yelled after her.

Christina stopped in her tracks and turned around, "What did you say?"

"I said I don't want Tina," he breathed. "But you said you wouldn't come to London with me as Christina."

She nodded. She remembered saying that.

"You didn't give me a choice," he continued. "You said you would only come as Tina. I'm a pig, but I wanted to have the job and you. I thought if I offered you the same job as my assistant in London then you could come and we could date longer, because... I wasn't ready for more." He ran his hand through his hair and started pacing the empty atrium. His footsteps echoed on the floor. "And I didn't think you were, either. But then you said I'd have to make a big sacrifice in order to even get Tina. I thought that meant you wanted me to ask you to marry me if you were going to come. And... What am I talking about? You two are the SAME PERSON."

Christina didn't know what to say. When she thought over their conversation it definitely seemed like a marriage proposal was what she was hinting towards. She colored because she wasn't sure that was what she meant.

"Anyway, I don't care," Mark said noisily. "We never get any time alone no matter how hard I chase you. There always appears to be someone waiting in the wings as soon as one of us has a few minutes. Even as we speak, Mindy and Trevor are on their way down and so we won't be alone in here for longer than a minute." He paused and took a deep breath. Then he said rationally, "I just thought if we moved to a city where neither of us knew anyone we might have a chance to actually get to know each other. But it's impossible. In London, I'll know Trevor and apparently, you'll know Dominic and he's going to be impossible to shake. And let's face it, wherever you go you are going to attract a string of admirers. And so now you're breaking up with me. Maybe that's well and good since I have no idea how to make you happy."

Everything he said surprised Christina. He sounded like he really wanted to be with her.

"Mark, we have so many problems," she said, trying to be sensible. "But let's deal with them one at a time. I have always felt you cared more deeply for me when I was pretentious than when I was sincere. That bothers me a lot."

Mark stopped pacing and faced her. "Are you trying to give yourself a multiple personality disorder? I mean really, both people are you. So, you don't want to be flirty and done up twenty-four-seven. Who could really blame you for that? But, when I first met you, you didn't seem fake to me."

Christina sighed, "That's because I really liked you."

Mark perked up like he was getting an idea. Then he said, "And on Valentine's Day when you flirted with Dominic? You were flirty then, too."

Christina dropped her hands in surrender. "That's because you were there and I knew you wanted to be out with me instead of Laura because you'd made a bid for me as well. So, I thought I'd make you jealous if I hung all over Dominic."

"So, if you act like that for those reasons, then what part of you is faking it?" he asked logically.

"But I—"

Mark interrupted, "You felt like flirting and you did. How is that pretentious? Just because you had the cover of being an escort, you didn't have to take responsibility for your actions. Did you tell yourself it was just for the job? Is that what caused all of this?"

"I don't know," Christina whined, frustrated. "I don't care. What I really want is for you to like me whether I decide to dress up to the nines or not, whether I decide to be all bouncy or if I want to be serious. I want to be smeared with mud and have you still think I'm cute."

"That's it?" he asked disbelievingly. "Done!" he exclaimed coming toward her and looking meaningfully into her eyes. "You are wonderful on your own. You're fun enough without the flare. Whether you're chucking your bra padding at me, or falling asleep with an open can of pop in your hand, or throwing underwear onto the highway—or whatever—whining, screaming, crying, sleeping—I want it all. Even when you're just sitting at your desk doing your paperwork, you are what I want. So, don't break up with me, Christina. I love you. Please give me a chance to work it out with you."

"You love me?" she gasped.

"Of course I do. I'm sorry it's taken me this long to say it," he said, pulling her hand to his heart. "I've loved you from the first. Just please, stop driving me crazy and stay with me."

Christina felt like she was going to cry, but she kept on being sensible and asked quietly, "What about London? That's the next problem."

"Do you want to go?"

"No," she said, allowing her head to droop.

"Then, that's all you needed to say. I won't go either," he said, kissing the palm of her hand.

"But, once-in-a-lifetime opportunities don't come along very often," Christina said, letting a tear slide down her cheek.

Mark cupped her face in his palm. "No. They don't," he said gently, looking at her like she was the once-in-a-lifetime opportunity he didn't want to miss out on.

"Okay, Mark. I'll stay. I won't quit," she said.

He pulled her into his arms and kissed her adoringly. Her hands were still on his chest and she felt his heart thudding madly against his rib cage. And for the first time, something miraculous happened. She felt like he really did love her for who she was instead of for who she wasn't.

"Do you think we should try to sneak past them," a soft voice said at the other end of the atrium.

"No," a male voice answered. "Let's wait until they're finished."

Christina thought Mark heard the voices, but he just kept on kissing her and making the world around her swirl. Christina could hardly pay attention to what they were saying, but through her daze, she could make out a little of their conversation.

"Well, if they made up then I should make some calls," Mindy's gentle voice said.

"Why?"

"Well, I was going to have some of my escort buddies come and help Christina save a little face since she was supposed to be brokenhearted tonight. You know, all my *male* escort buddies."

"You're a good friend," Trevor said kindly.

"No, I'm blood. There's nothing like developing a little bit of a mob mentality when your family's pride is threatened."

"I certainly know what you mean," Trevor chuckled. "But doesn't it look good to see them? When was the last time you were kissed like that, Mindy?"

"I don't really remember. It might have been yesterday, but I'll tell you one thing, it didn't take roots like that."

"I'll keep that in mind," Trevor said, right before Christina heard a gasp from the other end of the room.

She and Mark looked up to see Trevor kissing Mindy. Her cell phone had fallen onto the marble tile.

"Maybe they should do the commercial," Mark drawled before he kissed Christina again.

Chapter Eighteen

A Role

After all was said and done, Christina and Mark were back in the office on Monday, making eyes at each other across her desk. Two days later, Christina got fed up and moved her computer so it faced a different direction. How were they supposed to get any work done if they could see each other so easily? And because they were really part of the public relations department and not models, they had to do press releases and meet with members of the marketing department to make sure the launch of the new phone went well.

It was weird. When they went to the meetings where the pictures from their ad campaign were shown, everyone immediately recognized Mark and commented. No one recognized Christina. The first time it happened, Mark went to her rescue and told them she was the model he posed with, but afterward, Christina told him he didn't need to do that again.

"It looks like the company can't afford real models. Just let them think I'm a glamorous overpriced model and that you were drooling over me the whole time," Christina said flippantly. "That will make me happier. I don't like the questions about my hair and… face. Actually, it's kind of insulting that they don't think the girl in the pictures could possibly be me."

"That's why I have to make them understand how stupid they are," Mark responded.

"Whatever. Stop it. Tell them you're dating her. That will make them jealous and make you look like a stud. I can laugh at them in my sleeve, so everybody wins."

He rolled his eyes. "If you say so." Then suddenly, he remembered something and spoke up about it. "Hey, you haven't heard from Dominic lately, have you?" His tone was almost accusing.

"No. I haven't heard from him. I think he's afraid to mess with me since the night you gave him a fat lip."

Mark looked satisfied and went about his business. Pondering, Christina discovered she was quite curious about what happened to Dominic. Was he okay? Was he planning to sue Mark? He was quite capable of it. But days and weeks went by before she got the answer to her question from a most unexpected quadrant.

Mark was out of the office and Christina was left in her cubicle to tend to some of the mess that had stacked up while they were so busy. It was an ordinary day until Laura strode up to her desk.

"Hi Christina," the older woman said in a tone completely foreign to her. She almost sounded friendly.

"Hi," Christina said slowly. "How are you?" she asked. It is always the first thing you ask anyone when you work in PR. It was automatic when it came out of her mouth.

Laura smiled warmly. "I'm good."

"Is there anything I can help you with?"

"No. I just came by to see if you were interested in chatting with me while Mark's out," she said.

"Sure," Christina said. "We can use Mark's office. He's got clean chairs."

"Miracle of miracles! That must be your doing. He never used to have clean chairs. They used to always be covered with months of undone filing."

"You have a good memory. That was a while ago." Christina found her keys and opened the door for them. Inside, Mark had two chairs in front of his desk. Christina offered one of those to Laura and then sat in Mark's chair. "So, what do you want to chat about?"

"Mostly, I just wanted to offer you an apology."

"Why?"

She smacked her lips. "It's from Dominic because he feels terrible about the whole thing."

Christina didn't believe for a moment he felt anything other than irritation that he was out of the game. He just liked screwing around with her head and any other head that happened to be in the vicinity. Rather than explain that, Christina decided to humor his sister. "Does he?"

"Yes. He was worried about what would happen if he tried to contact you. I guess he and Mark had a little fight. But I'm like Dominic this way."

"What do you mean?"

"Dominic can't stand to apologize to you in person. He's too prideful, so he asked me to apologize in his place. I would like to apologize to Mark, but I can't do it, so I'm apologizing to you and I hope you'll pass it on," she explained.

"I can do that."

"Would you? Thanks. You're a sweetie."

Christina had never seen before how Laura could be related to Dominic or Alexander, but when she said those words it all came clear. She had never been interested in Mark. That was why she seemed so boring. She was bored. Maybe Laura wasn't as dull as a sugar spoon.

"So, if you don't mind me asking," Christina began. "Why did you chase Mark if you didn't like him? Just to make Collin jealous?"

"Nothing makes Collin jealous. He's not the jealous type. I only did it because Dominic kept insisting it would work eventually, but it wasn't one of his best ideas. I was on the verge of giving up on Mark when you showed up at the New Year's Eve party. Dominic took one look at you and decided I just had to chase Mark harder than ever. It was too bad I didn't realize he had ulterior motives. He just does such a good job selling his ideas."

Christina nodded. She certainly understood that.

"So, I'm sorry I interrupted your date with Mark at his apartment. It was really rude of me. That's my apology to you. And to Mark—I want to apologize for everything. I shouldn't have let myself get talked into messing around with anybody's feelings."

"It's okay. We're all learning that lesson this month. Did Dominic learn it?"

Laura straightened her back. "Dominic never learns anything except how to soothe his pride and land on his feet."

"Does that mean he's found a new model?"

"No. It means he's just landed Alexander a new cologne ad campaign in Paris."

"Impressive."

"Very. They're leaving next week." Laura popped open her purse and pulled out a business card. "Dominic wanted you to have this."

Christina took it and flipped it over in her hand. "The offer is still open," was written on the back in Dominic's very scratchy handwriting.

"Thanks," Christina said, as she put her hand under the desk and let the card fall silently into the trash can. "I owe you an apology, too. It was my idea for you to go on all those dates to get over Mark."

Laura looked confused. "Why?"

"They were with escorts."

"I know," she said smugly. "That was what convinced Collin to marry me. My dating Mark didn't bother him. Mark is a very respectable man. My going out with a male escort was a completely different matter."

"I thought you said he didn't get jealous?"

"He didn't. He got so angry it made his blood curdle, but he's better now. So am I. See? Dominic's plan to get Collin didn't work at all and yours worked perfectly."

"Thanks," Christina said. "But I didn't even know what the problem was."

"Well, what difference does it make? Everything worked out in the end."

"In that case, can you tell me what blackmail you had on Dominic that got him working for you?"

"Oh, it was nothing. Really. It was absolutely nothing," she said, dismissing it with a wave of her perfectly manicured hand.

Christina narrowed her eyes. "I'd like to know."

"Well, I suppose it doesn't matter," she said with an elegant shrug of her shoulders. "Dominic likes the escort situation. He doesn't always understand social constructs that don't have defined rules. When you have an employer/employee relationship, it's easier for him to get it to work correctly. Not for himself," Laura clarified. "He has hired Alexander's last three girlfriends."

"Why?"

"Alexander may be externally everything a woman wants, but internally, he's a crybaby. If he's left alone to manage his love life, he has extremely short relationships, sometimes measured in hours. If Dominic hires somebody, she gets a cut from Alexander's pay and she helps manage him. When the girl wants out, as all of them have, she leaves Lex a note and refuses to take his calls. He doesn't chase her because he's too selfish, and it doesn't matter anyway because Dominic is already in the midst of hiring someone new."

"That's a really dirty secret," Christina commented.

Laura smiled. "I think you can handle it." Then she got up. "Please ask Mark to forgive me. I hope we can meet without awkwardness the next time we have to… for work."

"I'm sure he'd be willing to do that."

"Excellent. I'll see you later. I have a lunch date with my husband," she said, still smug.

"Congratulations," Christina called to the retreating woman.

***

That evening, Christina had Mark over to her apartment for supper. She was making stuffed mushrooms and rice with a salad on the side. She had Mark chopping vegetables. She told him about her meeting with Laura.

Mark winced when he heard the last little bit about Alexander's love life. "That's very sad. No wonder he's bratty like that. He can't trust anyone around him. He must know what Dominic is cooking up behind his back, but he can't do anything about it if he's going to stay in business."

Christina was surprised. "Do you think Alexander knows?"

"Yeah. I do. I think that's why he wouldn't work with you. He knew you were someone Dominic recommended and that made you untrustworthy."

"He could have gone ahead with the shoot!"

"Maybe. But, think about it. It could have been that was the real job Dominic was trying to hire you for all along—Alexander's girlfriend," Mark said slowly.

Christina gasped. She hadn't thought of that.

Then he changed the subject. "It's good to know that no one is paying you to be with me now."

"I've got bad news for you. I'm getting paid."

Mark looked horrified. "Really?"

"Yep. You're paying me right now."

He chuckled. "How am I doing that? All this stuff came out of your refrigerator."

"Slave labor. After we're done eating, I'm going to make you help me with the dishes. There was no dishwasher in this apartment until you walked in. Get it? Now you understand how none of this is free."

"I guess it's true. If we were over at my place, I'd make you help me get the food ready, too. And I'd make you help clean up. I guess in that case, you'd be paying me to be with you."

"Absolutely. But then, you'd also be feeding me, so you'd be paying me to help you."

"Hm. So, how can I work it so that I'm not paying you?"

"There is no way," Christina said saucily as she pulled the vinegar from the cupboard. "You may as well just forget about it. You'll always be in debt to me."

He dropped his knife and swung around to face her. "Is that so?"

She nodded.

Looking into his playful brown eyes, she suddenly knew what he was talking about. It was how he wanted to get to know her, during quiet moments like the one they were having. It wasn't like that steamy encounter in the trailer, but a relationship built bit by bit. They didn't need to go to London to have it. It was available anywhere.

Or it would have been available anywhere if Mindy hadn't chosen that exact moment to enter the room. "What's for dinner? Did you make some for me?"

Mark sighed. "You know, I just might have to marry you to get five minutes alone with you."

"Well," Christina laughed. "Do what you have to."

The End

Dearest Reader,

Thank you for making it to the very last page of this book, and for reading this, my letter to you. Now that we've spent so much time together, I have something to confess. The truth is, I'm an independent novelist.

You might not think that's embarrassing, but it is. It means that I don't have a publishing company arranging for other authors to review my work so that I can look all posh on Amazon, Goodreads, etc. If you have a moment, could you do a poor little indie novelist a favor? Could you post somewhere, anywhere, that you enjoyed my book and recommend it to others? I'm not fussy. Anywhere people could see it will do. On Facebook, Instagram, Goodreads, Amazon, your blog, are all places that would do the trick marvelously. If I have to choose one I would prefer, I'd like Amazon reviews best. There are a lot of promotional sites that won't even speak to you if you don't have five reviews on Amazon. I would be ever so grateful.

If I can help out, please reach out to me. I'm on Facebook at svoauthor (where you could follow me if you wanted to know when my next book is coming out), and my blog address is http://stephanievanorman@blogspot.com.

Since you just finished a book, you might be looking for something new to read. If so I have a few recommendations. My other books available now are

Behind His Mask, Kiss of Tragedy, and *A Little Like Scarlett.* They're in print and ebook formats on Amazon if nowhere else.

Thank you, dearest reader, for allowing me to entertain you. I hope I can write for you again very soon!

With the Most Love,
Stephanie Van Orman

Made in the USA
San Bernardino, CA
03 December 2019